Snowed In with the Rancher

A Young Sisters Novel

Whitley Cox

PRINT ISBN: 978-1-989081-61-7

Cover artist: EmCat Designs

Editor: Proofreading by the Page

Beta-reader: Postive Proof Author Services

For Kristina.
Your friendship means a great deal to me.
Thank you so much for being wonderful you.
Love you

xoxo

Don't Forget

Be sure to sign up for my newsletter to stay up to date on new releases, deals and more.
Sign up here —> http://eepurl.com/ckh5yT

Become a Patreon Patron to get short stories, secondary character stories, favorite character update stories, exclusive cover reveals, exclusive excerpts from WIPs and more!
Support here —> https://patreon.com/authorwhitleycox

A few other books by Whitley Cox
The

Single Dads of Seattle

Grab book 1 here

https://books2read.com/HBTSD-SDS

*

The Quick Billionaires

Grab book 1 here

Quick & Dirty

https://books2read.com/QDirty-QBS

*

The Harty Boys

Grab book 1 here

Hard Hart

https://books2read.com/HH-HB

*

The Young Sisters

Grab book 1 here

Not Over You

https://books2read.com/not-over-you

*

Doctor Smug

https://books2read.com/DoctorSmug

*

Hot Dad

https://books2read.com/Hot-Dad

*

Snowed In & Set Up

https://books2read.com/SISU

*

Love to Hate You

https://books2read.com/Love2HateYou

Contents

1. Chapter One   1

2. Chapter Two   9

3. Chapter Three   16

4. Chapter Four   22

5. Chapter Five   31

6. Chapter Six   38

7. Chapter Seven   47

8. Chapter Eight   56

9. Chapter Nine   64

10. Chapter Ten   73

11. Chapter Eleven   82

12. Chapter Twelve   91

13. Chapter Thirteen   101

14. Chapter Fourteen   114

15. Chapter Fifteen   126

16. Chapter Sixteen   135

17. Chapter Seventeen   144

18. Chapter Eighteen   154

19. Epilogue   170

Chapter One

"Well that fucking sucks," Hannah said through the phone after Triss spent the last twenty minutes telling her friend how her boyfriend of three years had just dumped her out of the blue. "I'll certainly be leaving a scathing Yelp review at Lorne's restaurant now."

"Don't waste your time," Triss said with a sigh, flopping into her desk chair in her office. "The worst of it all is that I still live with the guy."

Hannah made a cringing sound. "Riiiight. How long did you sign your lease for?"

"Just a year, but we've only been there three months."

"Ugh. Awkward."

"And we were supposed to go spend Christmas with his family in New Hampshire, but he's taking *Echo* now."

"Wait, hold up—who the fuck is *Echo*?" Triss could just picture her raven-haired friend with the piercing blue eyes holding up her hand like she was a cop directing traffic and wrinkling her naturally thick brows in utter confusion.

"Oh, did I leave that part out? *Echo* is Lorne's culinary school girlfriend. They reconnected on social media a couple of months ago and that's why he dumped me. To get back together with her." Triss made sure her office door was closed before putting Hannah on speakerphone so that she could massage her temples with both hands. "And he'd like to move Echo into *our* apartment."

"So in other words, he wants you to move out?"

"Yeppers."

"Fuck almighty. Now I'm going to go and slash the motherfucker's tires, screw the Yelp review. Cut his brake lines, put his number on the wall in a men's bathroom at a biker bar for those looking for a good time."

"You'd never step foot into a biker bar." That brought a smile to Triss's otherwise perpetually scowling face. At least it felt like she'd been perpetually scowling since Lorne dropped the breakup bomb on her yesterday. But the thought of Triss's princess-esc friend with her designer everything going into the *men's* room of a sketchy biker bar was hilarious in its absurdity and gave Triss's lips the much-need lift at the corners they needed.

Hannah made a dismissive noise. "I would for you, babe. You know that."

Yeah, she did know that. Hannah was one of her closest friends. They met in grad school and although Hannah now worked in Manhattan as a speech pathologist, and Triss in Connecticut as a speech path, they spoke several times a week and made a point of getting together at least once a month for drinks, dinner, and more drinks.

"So now what are you going to do?" Hannah asked, the echo of other voices around her filtered through the phone. She had to be on the subway getting ready to head home for the day.

"For what? A house? A boyfriend? Christmas? Choose one. Their answer will be the same. *I have no freaking clue.*" It was times like these where Triss really wished she had a bottle of something stronger than sparkling water in the bottom drawer of her desk. Even a beer would be better than room-temperature sparkling water.

"Well, yeah, but I was going to say Christmas."

"No idea. I have no desire to go home and be the only kid at home with my parents. Besides, I think they're going to visit my mom's sister in Florida. Mieka is on a cruise ship doing her dancing thing, Oona is still in Montreal going to school. And then of course there is my oldest and youngest sister in Victoria, happy and blissfully in love. Gag. No thanks. As much as I love my niece and nephew, I don't feel like watching Pasha and Heath make googly fuck me eyes at each other. And Rayma has zero filter, so I'm sure she'd have no problem literally straddling her boyfriend and making out with him right in front of me."

"Yeah ... Rayma's a handful."

"Understatement of the century." It was also really funny coming from Hannah, since she and Rayma were a lot alike. Particularly in the lack of a filter department.

"Spend Christmas with me," Hannah said.

"Which is going to be where this year? Your family is spread out more than mine."

"I'm going to see my uncles in Colorado at their dude ranch and stud farm. They're grumpy, crotchety old buggers. Were in the Navy for a while, then bought a ranch when they retired from fighting bad guys."

"And why are you going there?"

"Because I can't stand to spend Christmas with my mother and her new husband, or my dad and his wife, who is five years older than me. And they can always use the extra help at the ranch during the winter. Plus, I love cuddling goats and baby horses."

"They have goats?"

"Dude ranch, stud farm, and petting farm, I should have said. They have it all. And I think they have a couple of mares that are getting ready to foal soon, so we might get lucky and get to cuddle some fresh babies."

"And these are your uncles?"

"Yeah."

Nibbling on her lip, Triss brought up a new window on her computer and punched in the website for her favorite discount airline. A flight to Denver wasn't *that* expensive.

And it wasn't like she couldn't deal with the Lorne and Echo stuff after Christmas when she got back. She'd been working crazy hours and long days for months since a lot of people had their therapy funding renewed in January, but the funding didn't roll over into the next year, so they were scrambling to try to use up their funds. Which meant that they were asking her to work extra sessions. It was good money, but it was exhausting.

"Go to your apartment tonight. Box up everything and I'll send my friend's moving company to go and grab it all," Hannah said.

"And take it where?"

"A storage locker for now? We'll spend the week in Colorado applying for new apartments. Worst-case scenario, you live in an Airbnb for a month. But it's not the end of the world."

No. It wasn't. But it still sucked.

"Fine," Triss said, glancing out the window at the snow-covered trees and ground. It was beautiful, and she'd always loved the snow, but she wasn't looking forward to having to move to a new apartment in it.

"I'm leaving Manhattan on the twenty-first, so plan to arrive in Colorado on the same day. I'll send you my flight itinerary and we can coordinate."

"I'm thinking maybe I should go see my parents for a night first, so I'll fly out of Baltimore. But I'll try to be there on the twenty-first, too." She found a flight that worked with Hannah's flight, since her very organized friend had already texted her the details, then before she could back out of the plan, she put in her credit card details and booked it. "You're sure your uncles will be okay with another person showing up?" Triss asked.

"They hate everyone, so it will make no difference."

Oh lovely. But that sentiment didn't actually bother Triss that much. She was in a pretty crappy, people-hating mood, too, and misery did love company.

"There! Done. Flight booked."

"Yay!" Hannah cheered. "This will be awesome. We'll get hammered, pot is legal in Colorado and I'm pretty sure my uncles smoke a *ton* of it, so we'll also get

4

high as fuck. We can just forget our worries and get fat because we'll constantly have the munchies. Then we'll go out to the barn and snuggle goats."

"I am due for a good goat snuggle," Triss mused with a smile.

"I haven't met a person who isn't," Hannah quipped. "All right, babe," Hannah whooped, "You, me and the goats in three days. Go home and pack and feel free to steal all of Lorne's shoelaces and dump out his favorite cologne. You have my permission to be petty and vindictive. It's allowed."

"I just want to get the hell out of there," Triss said, closing her computer, getting up from her desk, and shoving her arms into her coat.

"And you will. We will find you something way better. I promise. I mean, if we're being honest, Lorne was only an *okay* chef. There's a reason the guy doesn't have any Michelin stars or James Beard awards, let's just leave it at that."

"I'll see you in three days."

"Three days, baby. You, me, the goats and my crazy high uncles."

"Sounds like a Christmas to remember."

They disconnected the call and as Triss locked up her office, she caught herself smiling in the reflection of her colleague's door window. Maren's lights were off, so it turned the window into more of a mirror. Triss was smiling, and those lines around her eyes since Lorne dropped his bomb yesterday weren't nearly as deep.

Maybe a week in Colorado with a couple of old cowboys, her best friend, and some goats was exactly what she needed to find some perspective and sort things out.

And if she didn't find perspective or get anything sorted, at least she'd get in some goat snuggles.

"Good afternoon, folks, this is your captain speaking, we apologize for the delay, but the runway is finally clear and we are going to be landing in roughly thirty minutes. If you have any connecting flights, please know that most of the flights out and into Denver have been canceled due to weather. We apologize for the inconvenience, but your safety is our number one priority."

Crap.

What did that mean for Hannah's flight out of La Guardia?

Triss's flight had been delayed for three hours, then they circled and almost had to land in Utah because of the freak snowstorm that was hitting most parts of the country. But here she was, about to begin her descent into Denver and go spend Christmas with a couple of miserable old cowboys and their goats.

God, she hoped her friend's flight was not one of the ones to be canceled.

Up until she boarded, Triss and Hannah had been texting back and forth. Hannah's flight had been delayed, too, but she was already supposed to be leaving two hours after Triss. So now, Triss would have no way of knowing whether Hannah was still in New York or in the air, or if her flight had been rerouted somewhere else like Kansas or Ohio.

If Hannah's flight was canceled, did Triss even bother going to the ranch? Or did she just wait for a flight home to become available? She wasn't *that* far from her sisters in Victoria, Canada in the geographical sense of things, maybe she could just head north.

But that idea sat like a ball of habanero peppers in her gut.

Yes, she loved her sisters, niece, and nephew, but she was in no mood to watch them happily in love with their perfect lives and men. Not when Triss had been convinced that Lorne was her happily ever after just days ago.

Thank God she kept the receipt for the expensive watch she bought him. She returned it yesterday and bought herself a new pair of waterproof but stylish winter boots. They would keep her feet dry and warm, while also being fashion-forward.

Lorne hadn't even bothered to ask her where she was going or where she planned to spend Christmas when she spent two days packing up her life and painfully cohabitating with him while he was on the phone constantly with

Echo, reassuring her that he wasn't "cheating on her" with his girlfriend.

Ugh! Yeah, she'd rather spend Christmas with two crotchety veterans in Stetsons than another second with Lorne and the vapid Echo.

The plane landed, albeit with enough turbulence for the woman in the middle seat to dig her nails into Triss's arm as she held on and crossed herself at least twelve times. But they landed in one piece and that was what mattered.

As soon as they were allowed to, she turned on her phone to check her messages.

Nothing from Hannah. That had to be a good sign, right?

That had to mean that Hannah was in the air and set to land in Denver in a couple of hours.

Since it was nearly nightfall, and they had no idea how long it would take Hannah's plane to arrive, they decided that Triss would make her way to the ranch via a cab and Hannah would follow once she landed.

Once she grabbed her luggage from the carousel, she made her way outside only to find thick white flakes falling from the sky and a line of cabs nearly a mile long, but a line of people waiting for cabs nearly two miles long.

Great!

"Sir, sir, I will pay you triple your fare to just get me to where I need to go," Triss said, having handed the address to five taxi drivers and been turned down because of how out of the way the ranch was. "I do not care. I just need to get here in one piece, please."

The cabby, a man with no hair on his head but enough curly white hair for two heads flowing out over the buttons of his plaid shirt, scratched his chin, his fingers making a raspy sound on his scruff. "Triple?" He lifted a brow at her.

Triss nodded. "Triple. I just need to get there. Please."

His nod was reluctant, but he nodded nonetheless and heaved her suitcase into his trunk. She climbed into the backseat and exhaled a sigh of relief, removing her gloves and holding them in her lap.

She checked her phone, but there was no message or call from Hannah.

Thankfully, the cab driver didn't try to engage her in conversation.

Not that she wasn't a polite or friendly person, but Triss was exhausted and worried about her friend, the last thing she wanted to do was engage in small talk with a stranger who was going to be taking triple his normal fare just to do his job.

Whatever. Triss didn't care. She just needed to get to the ranch, then hopefully, Hannah's uncles would have some answers about Hannah or at the very least a stiff drink and a warm bed she could crawl into.

Chapter Two

"I'm going to have to let you out here," the cab driver said, pulling over to the side of the road below the snow-covered sign that read "Harris Brothers Ranch".

"What?" Triss exclaimed. "But I'm paying you triple. I need you to take me up to the house. The driveway up there is like half a mile long."

"And it hasn't been plowed or shoveled. I'll never make it down there, let alone back. Sorry." He popped open the trunk, climbed out, and heaved her bag into the snow.

Growling at this dick of a cab driver and her never-ending bad stream of luck, Triss flicked her gaze to the meter on the dash and grabbed enough cash out of her wallet for the jerk. He sure as hell wouldn't be getting a tip.

She pulled on her gloves, tugged her hood over her head, and stepped out of the cab. The cabby was having a smoke and eying her warily. "Still triple, lady."

She glared at the man through narrow eyes. "I'm aware." Thrusting the cash toward him, she gruffly took the handle of her suitcase from his hand. She wouldn't be able to roll it up the driveway, not with all the snow, so she was forced to carry the behemoth.

"Merry Christmas," the cabby called after her before he opened the door to his car, wedged his beer gut behind the wheel, and took off, leaving her in the dark and the cold and a half a mile from where she was supposed to be.

Grumbling and cursing the man's name, Triss began the trek through the snow toward the big farmhouse on the hill.

She checked her phone at least ten times between the road and when she finally reached the farmhouse with no lights on and the big dark red barn over to the side smelling of hay and manure.

"Where the hell are you, Hannah?" Triss muttered to herself as she yanked her suitcase up the steps of the wraparound porch toward the door. She opened the screen door and tapped the horseshoe door knocker three times.

It felt like ten minutes, but it was probably no more than two that she stood there in the cold and dark. She knocked again, this time five times and more forcefully.

If nobody was home, she would legit go find a horse stall to curl up in and cry.

Between Lorne, the delayed flights, the obnoxious cabby, and having to walk half a mile in the snow lugging her suitcase, Triss was not only dead on her feet physically, but also emotionally. The dam on her tear ducts was seconds away from breaking.

Footsteps echoed on the other side of the door and the porch light flicked on just before the big solid oak door was yarded open to reveal a shirtless man, not much older than Triss, wearing flannel pajama pants. He had abs for days, dog tags hanging between his pecs, a scowl on his face, and confusion in his dark blue eyes.

Was she at the right house?

Hannah said she was coming to spend Christmas with her uncles. This man could not be Hannah's uncle. Not when he should be on the cover of some firefighters with kittens calendar. Or in this case, cowboys with baby goats calendar.

His eyes traipsed down her body. "Who are you?" Dear God, his voice was exactly what she'd expect from a cowboy. Sex and rasp.

She swallowed, trying her hardest to keep her eyes on his face, not his six-pack. "I'm Triss. Hannah's friend."

His brows scrunched. "Hannah's flight had to turn around."

"Did it?" She checked her phone, though she realized the moment she did it that it wouldn't do her any good. Not only would Hannah not be able to text her if she was still in the air, but Triss's phone had up and died on her journey from the road. "Fuck," she muttered, stowing her phone back in her pocket. "Are you Hannah's cousin?"

He shook his head which caused the porch light to catch on a thick white scar on his chin and make it glow. "Uncle."

If the other uncle was just as young and hot, Triss was going to have a heart attack.

"She did tell you I was coming, right?"

He shook his head.

"Fuck."

"For Christmas?" he asked.

She nodded. "Yeah. Hannah invited me to join her here with you and ... your brother? For Christmas." At the mention of his brother, Triss tried to see around the man's big frame into the house and whether another one just like him was lurking in the shadows.

"Nate's in Texas. Took a yearling down there few days ago, got stuck in the snow."

"And you are?"

"Asher."

A man of very few words.

"Well ... uh ... I flew in from Baltimore. Hannah's my best friend and ..." She glanced back toward the road. "My cabby made me walk from the road. After I paid triple the fare to get here."

All Asher did was scratch at his bristly jaw, the sound of his nails on those short wiry hairs doing all kinds of strange things to Triss's lower belly.

Was he going to invite her in?

His eyes bore holes into her face for a solid thirty seconds, causing heat to worm through her until her hands grew sweaty in her gloves. Then, finally when she wasn't sure if he'd slam the door in her face or not, he opened it wider and stepped to the side. "Come in."

"Thank you," she murmured, awkwardly tugging her suitcase over the threshold and stepping into the dark, sparsely decorated farmhouse. It was warm inside, which she realized was from a wood stove in the corner of the living room. A window in the wood stove door was the only light in the room, its orange flames making the area around it glow.

She tugged off her gloves and removed her hood from her head, apologizing when a few droplets of water from it were flicked onto his hard chest.

"Guest room is down the hall. Bathroom is beside it," he said, jerking his scarred chin in that direction. Then before she could ask him any more questions, he turned away from her and padded his big bare feet up the creaky wooden staircase that led to darkness. A second later, she heard a door close, only then did she release the breath that had snagged in her throat when she saw that butt in those pajama pants.

Doing as she was told, she rolled her suitcase to a guest room next to a bathroom, opened the door, and flicked on the light.

Like the rest of the house that she'd seen so far, the room was tidy but minimal. There was a queen-size bed, an old wooden dresser, a nightstand on either side of the bed with metal desk lamps and that was it.

"Better than a snowy ditch," she whispered, fishing her charger out of her purse and immediately locating an outlet to plug in her phone.

As soon as it had enough juice, she turned it on, and what should pop up but a message from Hannah. *Sorry!!! They flew us to fucking Oklahoma! Oklahoma!!! I'm going to try to get there as soon as I can. Call me and let me know you're safe.*

Rolling her eyes, Triss did just that. It was past midnight, but she knew that

Hannah would be awake, and if she wasn't, she would answer her phone when she saw that it was Triss calling.

"I'm SOOOOOOOO sorry," Hannah said into the phone after the second ring. "I tried calling you as soon as I could. Where are you?"

"At the ranch," Triss said blandly.

"Oh shit, really?"

"Yep. You didn't tell them that I was coming."

"Whoops."

"You also didn't tell me that your uncle looks like a hotter version of Channing Tatum. What the hell, Hannah?"

Hannah snickered. "Whoops!"

"Is he really even your uncle? Are there two of them that look like this?"

"Yeah, he's my uncle. He's from my grandpa's second marriage. So he's like fifteen years younger than my dad. And his brother, my uncle Nate is a year younger than my uncle Asher. Uncle Asher is like … forty-two maybe. Something around that."

"And you didn't feel the need to mention this?"

"No?"

"Hannah!"

"What? You were just dumped, I'm not blind, I know he's nice looking. He's single and if you could end up being my aunt and we become legit family and not just best friends, then isn't that a win-win for both of us?"

"You planned this?"

"No. I did not plan to end up in mother-fucking Oklahoma for Christmas. I had every intention of being in Colorado with you and my uncles, but I did keep their attractiveness and age from you in order to get you to agree."

"*Uncle*. Just Asher." Triss said, sitting down on the edge of the bed and pulling off her boots. Her toes were warm and dry. Eat shit, Lorne!

"Where's Uncle Nate?"

"Texas. He drove down to deliver a horse and got stuck because of the weather."

"So it's just you and Asher?"

"I'm calling a cab first thing in the morning."

"What? Why?"

Triss put Hannah on speakerphone and went about getting undressed. "Because this is weird and awkward and not how I want to be spending my Christmas."

"So what are you going to do instead?"

Triss unbuttoned her skinny jeans and shimmied out of them. Just because her toes were warm from her boots, didn't mean her thighs hadn't been forced to endure the cold. They were bright red and slightly numb. "I have no idea." She'd already removed her coat, hanging it up on the hook on the back of the door, so she tugged her sweater over her head next.

"Then stay. I'll be there in a day or two, I swear."

"And until then, do what?"

"Cuddle goats and fuck my uncle? I don't know."

"Not helping!" Triss hissed, ditching her socks. "Get here ASAP, or I'm leaving and I might not tell you where I end up."

"You'd never do that. I'm the sister you never had."

"I have four sisters."

"Yeah, but none like me. And I have two brothers, so you're *definitely* the sister I never had."

"I'm looking at flights in the morning."

"Then make the most of tonight, Aunt Triss." The giggle in Hannah's voice had Triss rolling her eyes as she dug through her suitcase for her toiletries bag. "You're gross."

"I'm a realist. I don't want details. I don't need to know what positions you do it in, or what surfaces, or any of that shit, but Nate and Ash are more like my brothers or cousins than they are uncles. We grew up together."

"Still family, which makes it weird."

"Only if you subscribe to that kind of a family dynamic."

"Get your ass to Colorado, Hannah, I mean it."

"I will. I will." Finally, Triss's friend managed some remorse to her tone, though there wasn't much of it. "I'll call you tomorrow. Say *hi* to Asher for me."

"I'm pretty sure he's going to pretend I'm not even here."

"Impossible, baby, you're smokin' hot."

"Get here now!"

"I'm trying. Goodnight! Glad you're safe."

"Goodnight. Glad you are, too. Love you."

"Love you." Hannah ended the call, so Triss grabbed her pajamas, and having located her toiletries bag, she yanked open the door to her bedroom only to come face to face with the man her best friend wanted her to sleep with.

And of course, she was in nothing more than her underwear.

Fuck!

Chapter Three

"Uh ... towels," he said like an idiot, holding a stack of bath towels out toward the barely dressed stranger with the gold-flecked brown eyes.

She blinked those big eyes at him but otherwise didn't move.

He lifted the towels. "Here. There aren't any in the bathroom."

As if she suddenly realized that she was standing there in nothing more than a white bra and white panties, she closed the door, still not taking the towels, and a second later opened the door again, now wearing her dripping wet winter coat over her slender frame.

"Sorry," she said, taking the towels from his hands, their fingers brushing slightly underneath. "Thank you."

He grunted and nodded. "If you're going to shower, you need to crank the hot water all the way to full, then let it get scalding before you adjust. Old pipes." He turned to go, his cock having jerked in his pajama pants, making him realize he was barely dressed more than she was. And he didn't have any boxers on under his pants, so if he continued to have thoughts about her in her underwear, she'd know. "Breakfast is at seven."

"Uh ... thank you," she said again, before he started to climb the steps into the darkness toward the bedrooms upstairs.

He entered his room, closed the door, then slid into bed. But like fuck was he going to be able to sleep knowing she was downstairs naked and soaped up in the shower.

Who the fuck was this *Triss*? And what kind of a name was that?

She was beautiful, that was for sure. Those big brown eyes with long dark lashes, an almost olive skin tone, thick brown hair that hung in waves over her shoulders. Hannah hadn't said a fucking word about bringing a friend, and yet, he shouldn't have expected anything less. That was Hannah. Always with the surprises.

He'd be giving his *niece* a piece of his mind when he finally spoke to her.

But in the meantime, he had a gorgeous stranger downstairs in his guest room and bathroom and no idea what to do with her.

Though, he certainly had a few ideas of what he'd *like* to do with her.

Nate called him earlier before he went to bed to tell him that he was stuck in Austin after bringing the yearling down to its new ranch. Texas wasn't used to snow, so they had no idea what to do when it fell, leaving the state in a bit of a frenzy. He figured he'd be back in four or five days.

But that was four or five days of Asher doing everything on his own.

It was a full-time job when it was just the two of them on the ranch.

Fuck, it was a full-time job when they had their full-time ranch hands there, too. But everyone wanted to go see their family, so Nate and Asher figured they could handle a week by themselves feeding the animals and riding the fence lines to check for holes. Now, it was suddenly all on Asher and the snow was piling up.

Did he dare ask Hannah's friend to help out?

Not that he'd put her on a horse and send her out to ride the fence, but she could probably handle mucking stalls and filling troughs.

The squeal of the old pipes echoed through the house to let him know that she'd turned on the tap in the shower.

His cock stood at full attention as his imagination peeled away the white cotton panties and bra to reveal what was beneath, not that what she'd opened the door wearing left much to the imagination. And he'd always had a very active imagination.

Triss.

She'd paid triple the cab fair, then been forced to lug her gigantic suitcase all the way up the half-mile driveway, then bravely knocked on the door of a dark house and even then, she didn't ask to come in. It took him inviting her in. She had balls, he'd give her that.

Then again, she'd approached a dark house in the middle of nowhere and entered that house with a strange male she didn't know. Who had not been confirmed to be a relative of her friend. Maybe she wasn't as bright as he initially thought.

Not that he'd harm a hair on her head, but still. She didn't know that. And there were some seriously sick fuckers out there. He would know, he'd killed a lot of them.

The squealing pipes quieted down, but he could still hear the water running. Tucking his arms behind his head, he stared up at the ceiling. Then, because he knew that meddling little fuck would be awake, wherever she was, he grabbed his phone off his nightstand and shot off a text to Hannah. *A heads up about your friend joining us for Christmas would have been nice.*

She replied almost immediately because the woman lived on her phone. *What's the fun in that? She just got dumped by her dick of a boyfriend. Be nice.*

Interesting. Who in their right mind would dump a fox like Triss?

You know nothing about her. Psychos can be hot, too. She could have a shit personality and that was why the guy broke up with her.

Yeah, but she didn't strike him as the type to have a shit personality. And Hannah was an excellent judge of character. His niece wouldn't pick a person with a shit personality to be friends with, and she certainly wouldn't invite a person with a shit personality to his ranch. She knew better than that.

He texted her back. *Where are you?*

Again, she texted back right away. *Oklahoma. Earliest flight I could get to Denver was in three days. Feel free to hump my friend and cheer her up, though. ;)*

He growled, but his dick jerked at the thought of *humping* Triss. *Watch it, Hannah.* He texted back. *I'm still your uncle.*

Barely, she replied. *I mean, yeah, you are. But the age gap or lack thereof kind of muddies things and you know it. You have my permission to hump the heartbreak right out of Triss. Just don't break her heart in the process.*

"For fuck's sake." *Stop saying "hump"* he messaged back.

Bone? Fuck? Defile? Pick one.

Enjoy Oklahoma, Hannah.

Enjoy my friend Triss, Uncle Asher.

He put his phone back on his nightstand and tucked one hand behind his head while the fingers of his other hand found his dog tags on his chest.

His erection wasn't going anywhere, not when the shower was still running downstairs and Triss was still most definitely naked.

Could he take himself in his palm knowing a stranger was downstairs?

He'd certainly taken himself in less private places than his own bedroom. He'd also taken himself in the privacy of his own bedroom with a lot more people in the house.

There was just something about her ...

They'd spent all of five minutes—collectively—together and yet he just knew there was a reason besides his meddling niece and inconvenient weather that brought her here.

Hannah mentioned that Triss had just been dumped by her boyfriend. Why had he dumped her? Was she fragile and looking to cry? Or was she looking for rebound sex and to scrape every last memory of the idiot from her mind, body, and soul.

Asher could certainly help her out there.

He wasn't much for talking, anyway, but fucking he could definitely do.

Releasing his dog tags, he slowly trailed his hand down his abdomen and beneath his pants to where his erection pitched a tent. He began to stroke himself lazily, closing his eyes and picturing Triss with that long, dark hair wet down her back, her body soapy and silky soft and her hands running all over her skin, lingering extra long on her breasts—which filled out her bra nicely—and between her legs.

He'd only barely caught a glimpse, but her white panties had been slightly sheer and he could see a dark shadow behind the thin fabric. His mouth filled with saliva at the thought of getting to taste her there.

Fuck.

He picked up fervor with his strokes, squeezing the head of his cock as he reached the crown, then sliding back down to the base.

He sure as fuck wasn't going to pursue a hurt and healing woman, but if she wanted something, he also sure as fuck wouldn't turn her down. She just needed to know right off the bat that he didn't do relationships. He was married to this ranch and only ever would be. But after the chores were done, the animals were fed and the wood brought in for the wood stove, he could help her forget that douche that dumped her—at least until the storm passed.

His balls cinched up and he reached over to the nightstand for the box of tissues. He kept working his cock, the need to come building like a well-stoked fire in his lower belly. The water in the bathroom downstairs shut off and now he pictured Triss wet and naked, stepping out of the tub, her nipples growing tight from the cooler air hitting her. He'd like to suck those nipples.

"Fuck," he grunted, stroking himself even faster. He squeezed the crown even harder, pressure built in his balls and abdomen, and with his free hand, he grabbed a handful of tissues, rolled over to his side, yanked his pants down just enough to get his cock free, and blew his load into the Kleenex. "Fucking Christ," he murmured as he came, wishing it was Triss's pussy or her mouth he was filling with his cum and not a stack of tissues.

When he was done, he balled up the evidence and tossed it into the garbage can beside his dresser, then he went to the bathroom that he shared with his brother upstairs and washed his hands.

He thought about going back downstairs to make sure she had everything that she needed but decided against it. There was no need for him to check on her. She wasn't his *guest* and she was a grown-ass woman. If she needed something, chances are she'd figure out how to find it. He probably shouldn't have even bothered to bring her towels, since the linen closest was next to the bathroom door downstairs, but something had compelled him to give her the towels personally. He also could have just taken towels from the closet and put them in the bathroom for her, but he didn't.

On his way back from the bathroom, he stopped and stood at the top of the stairs for several heartbeats longer than he should have, staring down into the dark, waiting to hear the bathroom door open and her walk softly across the hall to her room.

Why?

He couldn't fucking say, but he did it anyway.

Softly, the door opened and it was all of four footsteps then she closed her bedroom door.

He stood there for five more breaths to see if she'd come out of her bedroom again, but she didn't. Shaking his head and berating himself for his stupidity, he returned to his room and closed the door.

Breakfast was at seven. Would she wake up for it? Would he see her before he headed out to work for the day? Did she like oatmeal?

21

Chapter Four

The time change had Triss waking up at five o'clock in the morning, despite the fact that she was bone-tired when she went to bed. Her body was conditioned to wake up early so she could do a workout in her living room, have a shower, then take her wholegrain toast breakfast sandwich with avocado, a fried egg, and turkey bacon with her as she drove to work. Then she stopped for a coffee from the Lebanese gentleman on the corner who made the best dark latte in Connecticut and walked into her office with her half-eaten sandwich and delicious latte from Ferjal. That was how she started her day every day.

She was a creature of habit, and it was hard to break that habit, even on the weekends. And since Lorne often worked on the weekends at the restaurant, Triss kept her routine up and went in to her office to work on files and programs.

Ferjal sold coffee seven days a week, why couldn't she work seven days a week, too?

Yeah, she definitely did not have a very good work-life balance.

Even though she was awake at five in the morning, she didn't immediately throw back the covers and go do calisthenics in a stranger's living room. She checked for flights on her phone for an hour, coming up with nothing since the storm had grounded all non-emergency flights for at least the next forty-eight hours. The weather app on her phone said it was still snowing and that they should expect even more snow over the next seventy-two hours. Yeah, if she wasn't going anywhere, she was going to stay snuggled up under the duvet for a bit longer, particularly since it didn't sound like Asher was awake yet.

Her mood was sufficiently soured when Lorne texted her asking where the Instant Pot was. Her reply of *In storage with all of my other worldly possessions since I was kicked out of my own apartment, of which my name is on the lease,* was not well received.

Lorne replied back with *Echo is very disappointed. I told her I had an Instant Pot and when she tried to find it to make a recipe she saw on Instagram, she was very sad.*

Well, whoopdy ding dong day. Echo was very sad.

But, Triss was a grown-up, so she replied with a very factual *The Instant Pot was a gift to me from my parents last year for Christmas. If Echo would like one for Christmas, I'm sure you still have time to run out and buy one for her.*

Lorne replied with his ever patronizing, *Real mature, Triss.*

She didn't bother responding after that. However, it didn't matter, that small bit of communication with Lorne was enough and the storm cloud over her head practically cracked with thunder as she stewed and steamed in her own anger under the covers.

With her phone in her hand and a sarcastic, bitchy comeback on her fingertips, she was about to tell Lorne where he could shove his far superior maturity when creaky floors and thin walls alerted her to Asher coming in the house from the front door at five minutes to seven. She hadn't even heard him come down the stairs, so he must have either been really quiet or done so before she woke up.

He probably went out and fed the animals.

Warmth bloomed in her chest at the notion of him feeding the animals before he fed himself. Despite his crusty exterior—which let's be honest, who wouldn't be cantankerous if they were woken up in the middle of the night and forced to let a stranger sleep in their house—she bet he had a soft heart.

Though, maybe he ate breakfast before he went out to the barn. But he didn't strike her as the type who would do that.

And all of two minutes with the man, thirty seconds of those minutes where you were in your underwear, has given you enough information to make that assessment.

She told her conscience to shut up and that she wasn't in the mood for its logic.

She needed something to take her out of this perpetually darkening mood. Something to ease the ache of her broken heart and soothe the sting of betrayal that felt worse than any bug bite she'd ever gotten.

She needed to cuddle a goat.

Slinging her feet over the bed, she was surprised to find the wood floor not chilly. That wood stove in the living room was doing a bang-up job keeping the house toasty.

She was in her flannel plaid pajama pants and a black tank top, so after throwing her mess of dark waves up into a top knot, she slid her feet into her slippers, opened her bedroom door, and headed toward the kitchen and the alluring scent of freshly brewed coffee.

His back was to her as he fussed at the counter, but she knew he knew she was there. His posture stiffened.

He had a black knit cap over his head that was still dusted with a few stubborn snowflakes that refused to melt, and a thick red and black plaid coat hung on his broad frame. His ass looked as delicious in a pair of well-fitting Wranglers as it did last night in his pajama pants.

She licked her lips.

"Cream's in the fridge if you don't take your coffee black," he said, not bothering to turn around, but rather just tilting his head toward it.

"Thank you," she murmured, scuffing to the fridge and opening it.

"You like oatmeal?"

"I do."

He grunted and plunked a mug of steaming black coffee on the counter.

She poured cream into her coffee and picked up the mug, cradling it in both hands and bringing it up to her chest to let the steam waft up her nostrils and wake her up.

Leaning against the counter, she watched him as he worked.

He had bacon frying in a pan, only four strips, and four eggs frying in another pan. Oatmeal sat steaming in two bowls and he had a bottle of sriracha hot sauce and a bowl of grated white cheese in his prep station, as well.

"Do you uh ... need help today?" she asked, gingerly taking a sip of her coffee and having to suppress a moan from just how good it tasted. The man knew how to brew a good cup of Joe.

Not bothering to answer her, he flipped the eggs out of the frying pan and into the bowl of oatmeal, then he crumbled the bacon on top of the eggs, added cheese, sriracha and finally salt and pepper. Her mouth watered.

He turned around, finally showing him her face, and handed her the oatmeal. "Help on the ranch?" he asked, going to sit down at the head of an old but well-built wooden table.

She joined him, taking a seat one chair down from where he sat. "Yeah. I checked flights and the weather and I'm sorry, but, I'm not going anywhere for at least forty-eight hours. Probably closer to seventy-two. I don't want to be a bother, so I'd like to help in any way that I can. I know this wasn't how you saw your Christmas going. Spending it snowed in with a stranger. I certainly never expected to be snowed in with a cowboy."

"Rancher."

She lifted her head, her full spoon paused in the air. "Pardon?"

"I'm not a cowboy. I'm a rancher. This is a stud farm and dude ranch." His nose wrinkled. "And petting farm, I guess, too."

Nodding, she rolled the word around in her head for a moment, then said, "Sorry, rancher. I never expected to be snowed in with a rancher for Christmas."

"What can you do?"

I can climb into your lap and wipe that scowl off your face. Why did her brain immediately go into the gutter?

"Any experience working with farm animals?" he asked, tucking food into his cheek and chewing.

She shook her head. "I'm afraid not. But I'm a fast learner and have no problem getting my hands dirty. If you want me to muck stalls or ... or ... I don't know what else there is to do, but I have no problem doing it."

A tight, barely discernible smile lifted on one corner of his mouth. "Ever been on a horse?"

She shoveled some of the delicious savory oatmeal into the mouth, so all she could do was nod. "I have," she said with a smile, after swallowing. "I went to ranch camp one summer when I was a kid. My best friend wanted to go, but my parents couldn't afford it since I'm the second oldest of five girls, so my friend's parents paid for me to go as a birthday present for me. It was two weeks of riding horses, brushing them, feeding them and it was so much fun."

He snorted, but it didn't seem like a cynical kind of snort. "Ranch camp, huh?"

"Yeah. Each kid got assigned a horse for the week and my horse's name was Indiana. She was beautiful, very gentle—a blonde Tennessee Walking Horse if I remember—and I swear I could have sat there and stroked her velvet nose for the rest of my life."

A softness creased his eyes and he took another bite of his oatmeal. "How'd you say you know Hannah?"

"We met in grad school. I'm a speech path, too, but I live in Connecticut and she, well, you know she's in Manhattan."

He nodded but didn't say anything. She'd already realized from last night that he was a man of few words, it didn't matter whether he was woken up from his sleep or not it seemed. If he didn't have to speak, he didn't.

Whereas Triss was a talker. She always had been. Silence made her nervous.

She felt like people we judging her when they were quiet, particularly when they were quiet and looking at her—like Asher was.

So she filled that quiet with chatter.

"I mean, if you'd rather keep a one-summer-ranch-camp kid like me out of your barn, I'm happy to cook in here. I'm no Nigella Lawson, but I can roast a chicken over a beer can almost better than anybody." She grinned and sipped her coffee.

"Who the fuck is Nigella Lawson?"

"A celebrity chef out of England."

He grunted, stood up, and finished his coffee, taking his empty plate with him to the dishwasher.

Man, he ate fast.

She scrambled to finish her own breakfast and stood up to put her dishes with his in the dishwasher.

"Meet me in the barn," he said, his voice like honey-coated gravel as he stood almost toe to toe with her, his eyes raking her body and causing flames to ignite along her skin wherever his gaze touched. "Once you're dressed."

She nodded eagerly. "Thank you. I'll go get dressed right now."

She finished her coffee, put the mug in the dishwasher, then practically skipped down the hall toward her room excited to distract herself from her heartbreak and also cuddle some goats.

Triss brushed her teeth, hair and was dressed in under six minutes. She figured Asher would already be in the barn, so when she found him in the kitchen filling up two thermoses with coffee and adding cream to one of them, she was surprised, but also delighted.

"Here," he said, handing her the thermos he'd just added cream to.

"Thank you." She accepted it from him and followed him to the front door where they pulled on their coats, gloves and boots. She'd brought hers out of her room with her earlier.

"You got a hat?" he asked her, pausing to glance at the top of her head, his hand on the doorknob.

She tugged her hood over her head. "Will this do?"

With an eye roll, he shook his head. "No." Then he pulled off the black knit cap he'd had on his head and tugged it down over hers, since she'd released her hair from its top knot and plaited it into a thick Dutch braid down her back. Then he reached into a wicker basket on a shelf over the coat hooks, pulled out a navy blue kit cap, and yanked it over his head. "Keep your ears warm."

She followed him out into the yard where fat, white flakes fell from the sky. The ranch looked so different in the daylight than it did at night.

She hadn't realized how enormous the land was, or how many outbuildings there were, either.

A whinny and a bray from the barn made goosebumps of glee prickle along her arms.

"Hannah said you guys have goats?" She had to pick up her pace to keep up with his long, purposeful strides. Even though the snow was practically up to her knees—only Asher's ankles since the guy had at least six inches if not more on her—he still walked fast and sure.

"Ten," he said with a grunt. "More in the spring when they have kids."

"Well, Hannah won me over when she told me I could cuddle goats if I came here, so ..."

He craned his neck around to look at her, his brow lifting up on the right side until it disappeared beneath the cap. "Cuddle goats?"

Triss shrugged. "Isn't that what you do at a petting farm?"

"If they allow it," he said, turning back around and continuing to walk toward the barn. He heaved open a side door and stepped inside. The place was heated and smelled like fresh hay and fresh manure. Some people hated the smell of manure, but Triss didn't mind it.

Over a dozen giant horse heads appeared along the long walkway, the residents apparently smelling a newcomer and wanting to check things out.

Immediately, she abandoned Asher and went to the sandy-colored horse with the straw-like mane. "Well, hello, gorgeous," she said, pressing her forehead to the horse's forehead and petting its cheek.

"That's Greenleigh," Asher said, coming up behind her.

"Hello, Greenleigh. Aren't you a beautiful girl?"

He cast her one of those half-hitched smiles. "Had twins this past summer."

She patted Greenleigh's neck before reaching up to scratch her ears, which made the horse bend her head to give Triss better access. "Well done, Greenleigh. One foal is impressive enough, but two. What a good mama."

A brown horse beside Greenleigh's stall was making snuffly noises and bobbing his head.

"You give one attention, you gotta give it to 'em all," Asher said, patting the brown horse's neck. "Macklin is an attention whore and won't let you leave until you show him the same amount of love you did Greenleigh ... times ten."

Triss's mouth opened in shock. Those were probably the most amount of words Asher had strung together since she arrived.

Clearly, he felt most in his element and comfortable out here with his horses.

Patting Greenleigh on the neck once more, then kissing her cheek, Triss made her way over to Macklin the attention whore. He immediately started nuzzling her, bopping his head into her chest and face for affection, which had Triss laughing. "Easy, Macklin, we only just met."

"He doesn't care," Asher said with a slight chuckle to his tone.

Triss giggled again when Macklin butted her with his nose and dipped his head so she could reach his ears.

"If you want snuggles, forget the goats. Macklin will literally try to climb into your lap if you sit down with him." Asher handed her a couple of carrots from a bucket and she fed them to the brown-eyed Macklin.

When she moved on down the line to the next horse, Macklin made a snort of discontent. "I'll be back for more, Macklin, I swear," she said, laughing.

"This is Hula-Hoop," Asher said, introducing her to the sleek black mare in the stall next to Macklin's. "And that beside her is Dare."

She gave attention to Hula-Hoop, then Dare. Eventually, after well over an hour, Asher had introduced her to all the horses in the barn, as well as the goats which weren't nearly as keen on cuddling as she hoped. There was also a donkey named Sasquatch, a pony named Magic, and two very old miniature horses named Frodo and Sam.

"I'm sure I'm going to forget some of their names," Triss said, feeding the last carrot in the bucket to Magic, then wiping her hands on her jeans and turning to Asher, her grin wide. "When is ... shit ... is it Pom-Pom that's pregnant or Carolina? See? I told you I'd forget their names."

"It's both," he said, stowing the bucket under a workbench. "But Carolina is due any day now."

"Oh that's exciting."

He grunted, reached for a shovel and handed it to her. "You said you're okay to muck stalls?"

With a grin she couldn't wipe off her face even if she tried, she accepted the shovel. "I will gladly shovel shit if it means I get to hang out here longer." Then, ignoring his bewildered expression, she went back to Macklin and kissed his cheek. "Especially with this handsome fella."

Chapter Five

Who was this woman?

First of all, she didn't know how to shut the fuck up, but second of all, she *liked* shoveling shit?

Asher had had a few women in his life since he and Nate bought the ranch, but not one of those women had been keen to muck stalls.

Of course, they did it, but they complained about it the entire fucking time.

It was only the ranch hands or those who boarded their horses at the ranch that did it without complaint. A few well-off families in the area who bought their kids a horse, but didn't have a place to keep it, rented stall space from Asher and his brother and boarded their horse here. It was extra cash in their pocket and wasn't that much more work. A lot of those kids—mostly teenage girls—offered to help out more, as well, and for a reduced rate on boarding, Asher and his brother got cheap labor.

But Triss mucked stalls and shoveled shit almost with gusto.

Asher led each horse out of the stall and into the covered and heated corral so that Triss could clean the stall. He only had four horses out at a time, since not all his tenants got along.

The Mustang at the end—Mercy—was a bit of a dick, so they saved him for last and gave him the corral to himself. Which Mercy loved because he got to run around like an asshole.

"He's beautiful," Triss mused as they stood there and watched Mercy prance and run around the corral.

"Yeah, he's also worth almost half a million dollars. But he's a dick."

Her soft brown eyes with the gold flecks nearly popped clean out of her head. "Half a million dollars for a horse?"

Asher snorted. "A lot of stallions are worth *over* a million if they're from good breeding."

"And he is?"

"He's getting to be. Lineage isn't long enough yet to command that kind of money, but his foals foals will. He's just such a jerk, though. Nips at some of the other horses. Hard as fuck to collect from him. Seems to hate me in particular."

"Collect wha—" He lifted his eyebrow at her and that cut her off. "Oh! You do that?"

"We do. And he's way too fucking rough to put him with a mare and try it the natural way. He could kill her."

"Jeez. So the reason he's not worth a million is that you can't get him to procreate because he's such—"

"An asshole, yeah. Nate's the horse whisperer, not me. If anybody can get that horse to heel, it'd be my brother."

"And he hasn't been able to?"

Asher shook his head. "Haven't had Mercy long enough for Nate to work his magic. Horse only arrived a couple of weeks ago. Then Nate had to go down to Texas to deliver that yearling."

Fuck, now he was as bad as Triss with the chit-chat.

But she just kept asking questions and as much as he hated talking, it was easiest when he was out here in the barn and with the horses. And as long as she kept her questions about the horses, then he had no real issues answering them. Besides, he liked her company. The horses took to her right away, particularly

Macklin, though, he wasn't picky about where he got his affections. But she gave them all attention and the smile on her face as she spoke to them was real and had him smiling, too.

"So if you can't ... jack off the horse for lack of a better term, what will you guys do with him?"

"Sell him, I guess. But we wouldn't get what we paid for him. Not with that temperament."

She nibbled on her lip and a warm, fuzzy feeling spread in his lower belly. "Hmm," she hummed, her gaze tracking Mercy in the ring. "He's just so pretty. He needs to have babies. Who would you breed him with?"

"Ideally, Piccadilly, but he'd definitely kill her if he mounted her. Callie and Hula-Hoop, too."

His stomach grumbled. They'd been out in the barn for hours shoveling shit, feeding horses, and keeping Fumble the goat with a penchant for mischief from escaping. He'd done it three times in the course of three hours and they could not figure out how he was getting out.

And as if he knew Asher was thinking about him, a *mehhh* from the other side of the corral had them pivoting their gaze from Mercy to the stupid fucking goat that had somehow entered the corral with the demon horse.

"What the fuck?" Asher barked, running around the corral to the closest point where the goat was. "This goat's got a death wish."

Mercy had already spied the stupid goat and was trotting over toward it, his nostrils flaring, head swishing back and forth and causing his black mane to whip around.

"Don't kill the goat," Asher yelled at the horse, who obviously didn't understand a single word, since he was proving almost impossible to train.

When he was closer to Fumble, Asher leaped over the side of the corral and went to grab the goat, but of course, Fumble thought they were playing and did a little goat side-hop away, then ran in that goat-like two legs at a time way away from Asher.

"Fuck!" he barked.

He wasn't even paying attention to Triss, since there wasn't really a way that she could have helped anyway, but when he heard a *snick snick* of someone clicking their tongue in their cheek and Mercy lifted his head, dread pooled like an icy river in his gut.

Triss was in the corral with Mercy and Mercy's attention was now on her and not Fumble.

"What the fuck are you doing?" he bellowed, running toward her, while Fumble bleated and ran around like an idiot-stick. "Get out of here."

She ignored him, held up her hand, and called Mercy again. Her eyes only cast sideways to him briefly and she shook her head just barely. Asher stopped in his tracks so fast he sent up a small cloud of dust.

He knew better than to run at a horse, what was he thinking?

He was thinking he needed to get this city slicker out of the warpath of the murderous Mercy.

Mercy slowed down his trot as he approached Triss and simply walked the last few feet toward her, his nostrils flaring as he exhaled deeply.

Worry spun in Asher's stomach. Two weeks at ranch camp and a morning mucking stalls and feeding horses carrots was not nearly enough fucking experience to be getting into a corral with an asshole Mustang. What was she thinking?

Mercy blinked several times, snorted, pawed at the ground twice with his right hoof, then he dipped his head and pressed it against her open palm.

Holy fuck.

Her smile was radiant.

She reached her hand up and scratched between Mercy's ears, which prompted the horse to head butt her and demand more. She giggled and started to scratch him with both hands.

Slowly, Asher approached her and Mercy.

"That was dangerous," he said, his tone harsher than he intended it to be. "And stupid, and foolish, and reckless and—"

"It worked," she said, cutting him off and leaning her forehead against the side of Mercy's head, then kissing his cheek.

Asher reached out tentatively to stroke Mercy, but the horse snorted again and backed away from him.

"Jesus, buddy, okay. I got it. You don't like me. Message received." He held up his palms and gave Mercy and Triss the space they needed. "That was still reckless, though," he said, eyeing her as she pressed kisses to Mercy's black nose.

"I know. But sometimes we have to take risks in order to get what we want, right?" Her gaze flicked to his and something burned in the gentle brown, something almost primal and it made his entire body ignite with flames. But they weren't anywhere near hot enough to burn away his anger at her for doing something that could have gotten her hurt, or even fucking killed.

With a grunt, he turned around. "Now I need to get that fucking goat." Then he went after Fumble, who seemed to laugh at him every time Asher lunged, then Fumble dodged, sending Asher crashing face-first into the dirt. It took lassoing the damn animal and tying him up in his stall before Asher felt comfortable enough leaving the barn to head in for a late lunch.

"Is it already two o'clock?" Triss marveled as they walked toward the house, snowflakes catching on her nose and eyelashes. "Time just flew."

He grunted again, opened the door to the house, and let her inside ahead of him.

"I'm happy to make lunch if you like," she offered, stepping out of her winter boots and hanging her coat up on the hook beside his. She kept the knit cap on her head and went to set her gloves next to the wood stove.

He didn't bother to say anything to her, just followed suit and added more wood to the fire, as well.

Assuming his silence was a confirmation, she was already in the kitchen with bread and cheese out. "Grilled cheese and tomato soup sound good?" she asked, having also found the Campbell's Soup cans in the pantry and grabbed two.

He grunted and turned down the dampers on the wood stove a bit.

"Are we back to the grunting?" she mused, a chuckle in her voice as she showed him her back and went about making lunch in his kitchen like she belonged there.

Why did that rub him the wrong way, but also make something grow tight in his chest?

He didn't say anything, didn't even stay in the room. Instead, he took the stairs two at a time, needing some space from the woman who had shown up on his doorstep last night and was now humming in his kitchen.

What the fuck?

He pissed in his bathroom and washed his hands, placing both hands on the sink, he leaned over and studied his face in the mirror.

The white scar on his chin seemed whiter and more prominent than normal. His doctor had offered to make a referral to a plastic surgeon for him to see what could be done to make the scar less visible, but Asher didn't care enough.

He didn't care how it made him look, anyway. Nate said it made him look more badass. Asher couldn't give two shits. What he did hate was that when he looked at himself in the mirror, that scar was a constant reminder of what had happened. It brought him back to that day like it was almost yesterday.

His knuckles ached. He glanced down at his hands gripping the pedestal sink and had to almost pry his fingers loose, they were so tight.

This isn't Iraq. This isn't Syria. You're home in Colorado on the ranch. You are not there. You are home. This is home.

He closed his eyes and breathed deeply. In through the nose, out through the mouth. Over and over again until his heart rate steadied and the cramps in his fingers were gone.

It'd been over five years since he and Nate AKA Blaze had retired from their special operative team. They used some inheritance money they got from their mother's brother to buy the ranch, having worked with their uncle on his ranch their entire childhood.

Both Asher and Nate—his nickname on their team was Blaze, so they were

Ash and Blaze—were pyrotechnic and weapons specialists. They'd taken every course out there on bomb training—how to make them and how to defuse them—and also trained others to do the same.

But it didn't matter how many thousands of hours Asher had under his belt of training and experience, when a bomb was dropped on a hospital from the sky in Iraq, your skills in defusing it are worth jack shit.

The only reason he was still alive was that he'd been walking to his Jeep after dropping off one of his fellow soldiers to get stitched up. Mauricio forgot his phone in the Jeep, so Asher said he'd go grab it so Mauricio could call his wife. Then the bomb was dropped, Asher dove under his Jeep and watched as the hospital and everyone in it was burnt to a crisp. Sometimes, he could still hear their screams.

He touched his chin. He'd taken a piece of metal to the face, resulting in the scar. That was his only injury.

Every person in that hospital died. He was the only survivor.

Yeah, a lot of good all that training did him that day.

He gave himself another full minute before he splashed cold water on his face and returned downstairs only to hear his niece's voice on the phone saying that she was in the hospital.

Chapter Six

"It's nothing," Hannah said for the millionth time. "I'm fine. Plus, my doctor is like crazy-hot, so I'm not itching to leave."

"Tell me again how it happened," Triss said, paying little mind to Asher when he entered the kitchen, worry creasing his handsome face.

"I slipped on some black ice on the crosswalk leaving my hotel to go grab something to eat at the diner across the street. Broke my ankle and cracked my hip. I'm like a ninety-year-old woman, I guess."

"Osteoporosis does run in the family," Asher said, his deep voice gritty and edged with concern.

"Oh hello, Uncle Asher," Hannah said with sarcasm in her tone. "Yes, mom has already lectured me on the importance of taking calcium and vitamin D."

"So what's the diagnosis?" Triss asked, ladling steaming tomato soup into two bowls. "Do you need surgery?"

"No. The cracked hip isn't enough to warrant surgery. I just can't move for you know ... ever again, or at least until it heals. And my ankle is in a cast. But they think I can get one of those walking casts soon. It was just a hairline fracture."

Triss flipped the grilled cheese sandwiches onto plates and carried them over to the table, smiling shyly at Asher before returning to the counter to grab the plate of apple slices she'd cut up.

"I've already called Uncle Nate and he's going to take a detour on his way up from Texas and pick me up. No sense flying home to my apartment in Manhattan when I can't do anything for myself anyway. So I might as well come to you guys and have you wait on me hand and foot, right?"

Triss and Asher snorted at the same time, their gazes locked for a long, awkward moment before he averted his eyes and picked up half a sandwich.

"Maybe go to your mother's?" Asher offered, though his tone said everything. They all knew that Hannah's mother had absolutely zero maternal instincts and even in her compromised state, Hannah would somehow end up catering to her mother and taking care of Wynonna rather than the other way around.

"You're *hilarious*, Uncle Asher. I've always said of all my uncles, you're the funniest," Hannah quipped, everything she said dripping with sarcasm.

"I'm going to tell Nate you said that." Asher dunked his sandwich into his soup.

"So I'll be there when Nate gets there." She paused for a moment. "Triss, take me off speakerphone, please."

Triss did as she was asked and put the phone to her ear. "What's up?"

"You bone my uncle yet?"

Triss's face flooded with heat and she abruptly got up from the table and wandered into the living room, bringing her voice down to a forced whisper. "Hannah, knock it off."

"What?" Hannah whined. "It was just a question. And I could have asked it while I was still on speakerphone."

"And I would have died from embarrassment and you would be a murderer, so it's a good thing you didn't."

"You're so dramatic. I told Asher he has my support to hump away your heartbreak, so he knows ..."

"Knows what?" Triss yelled into the phone, forgetting that she'd been whispering.

"That you're available and expecting to be humped into happiness."

"Quit saying *humped* and oh my God. Why would you do that?"

"Because you're sad, he's lonely, why not kill two miserable birds with one stone and set them up together? Besides, I'm not going to be having any sex for a while with this busted old lady hip, so—"

"You're going to live vicariously through me sleeping with your uncle? Do you have any idea how messed up that is?"

"Hmm ..." Hannah mused. "Yeah, when you put it that way, it kind of is. But I still support the union, even if I can no longer live vicariously through your vagina."

"I'm hanging up now, you psychopath."

"Love you, too."

"Love you. Behave."

"I never do. Tell Asher I love him, too."

"Goodbye." Then she hung up and stared out the living room window at the snow-covered field, her eyes wide, face on absolute fire.

Hannah had given Asher permission to *hump* her. What the hell?

And so now, Asher knew that not only had Triss been dumped by her boyfriend but that he was supposed to have sex with her? Could this get any more awkward?

Did she even want to ask that question? Or should she just walk out into the blizzard without a jacket on and not stop until she got hypothermia, fell asleep, and died in the field. That would probably be less painful than dying of utter embarrassment, which was most likely how she was going to go, and quickly, too.

"Soup's getting cold," Asher said, his voice a deep, throaty rumble that had her nipples pebbling beneath her black T-shirt. Oh yeah, and she'd gone with a pad-free bra today, too, so her headlights were on for everyone—which meant

Asher—to see.

Inconspicuously, she rubbed her arms over her chest to get her nipples to soften, but it barely worked, if anything, she liked the friction a little too much, and her pussy clenched.

When she figured her nipples weren't going to cut glass anymore, she turned around, plastered on a stupid smile, and joined him in the kitchen.

"Everything okay with Hannah?" he asked, dunking another sandwich half into the soup.

"Physically? No. Mentally? Also no." She grabbed a sandwich half and dunked it into the soup.

Asher snorted a laugh. "She's a meddler, that one."

Even if the soup wasn't lukewarm, but scalding hot, it would be no match for how Triss's cheeks felt. She could probably fry an egg on them.

Did Asher notice? She usually went bright pink when she blushed and if the heat in her cheeks was any indication, was probably as pink as a stick of bubble gum right now.

"Don't do anything like that again," he said after several long moments of silence passed between them as they ate lunch.

"Do what? Answer the phone? Walk out of the room while on the phone?"

His glare was impatient and bordering on rude. "Get in the corral with a horse like that. It was dangerous, reckless, stupid and you could have gotten hurt."

She rolled her eyes. "But I didn't. Mercy just needed a bit of patience and I gave him that."

"Suddenly you're the fucking horse whisperer?"

"No, suddenly, I'm a new person at this ranch who he doesn't know and who has the patience he deserves and wants. I'm not trying to usurp you as top dog or any of that shit. I know this situation is weird. You don't know me, I don't know you, but I'm trying to make the best of a bizarre situation. I offered to help and I meant that. I don't just sit on my ass while others work. That's never been my style." She finished the first half of her sandwich and grabbed the second,

41

dunking it once again in the soup.

"Mercy is unpredictable," he said. "Don't get in the corral with him again."

With her free hand, she saluted him. "Sir, yes, sir."

The thundercloud over his head quadrupled in size and lightning practically cracked overhead.

Well, now he felt how she felt when she woke up this morning. The difference was, she was trying her damndest to get out of her foul mood, doing whatever she could to distract herself, whereas he seemed content with the storm over his head.

The only time he'd been even remotely *pleasant* was when they were outside with the horses. He'd actually conversed with her, strung more than six words together and he'd smiled. And when that man smiled—holy shit.

His soup bowl was empty, his sandwiches gone. He hadn't touched the apple slices, but stood up anyway and took his dishes to the dishwasher. "I can handle the rest of the day myself," he said, leaving zero room for negotiation.

"Am I being punished for trying to help?" She didn't bother to stand up, but rather sat there eating her lunch, waiting for the beefy rancher to either answer her or have an aneurysm. Based on his expression, he really could go either way.

"If I was *punishing* you, Triss, you'd know," he replied, his voice dark and causing warm tendrils of desire to spin through her. The glint of something wicked and wild sparkled in his midnight-blue eyes, but it was gone a second later.

She swallowed and licked her lips. "I'm sorry. I won't do anything reckless like that again."

His brow lifted, then his shoulders slumped as he sighed. "I'm riding the fence to look for holes, you can come if you want." Showing her his back, he put his dishes in the dishwasher and began to fill the sink with water in order to scrub the pan and pot.

Triss bounced a little in her seat as she took another bite of her sandwich. She had no idea what "riding the fence" meant, but she was excited to do it anyway.

Because if she stayed cooped up in this house with nothing to distract her, it would be her lonely broken heart that would inevitably try to keep her company, and she still had that itchy finger that wanted to send mean, immature texts to Lorne.

Riding the fence looking for holes was exactly what it sounded like it was. They rode their horses in the snow along the fence line looking for holes. Then, if they could, they patched up the holes.

Asher rode his horse Dare, while he put Triss on Hula-Hoop. She couldn't say that it was exactly like riding a bike—a skill which you're never supposed to forget once you've learned how to do it—but she wasn't as much of a beginner as she expected herself to be, either. A lot of what she'd learned at ranch camp nearly two decades ago did come back to her, and even though she knew her ass and thighs would be sore tomorrow, she wasn't struggling to ride, either. She bounced with the horse, used her legs, and within ten minutes she and Hula-Hoop were riding merrily behind Asher and Dare down the fence line.

The snow was still falling, but the flakes were quite a bit smaller and less dense. The wind, however, had picked up and was hitting them all right in the face so that it felt like they were being bombarded with ice pellets as they went.

"I'm sorry, baby," Triss said, bending forward and petty Hula-Hoop's neck. "I'll give you extra carrots and snuggles when we get back to the barn. I know this can't be fun for you, either."

"Could have stayed inside," Asher said, climbing back up onto Dare after having repaired a part of the fence.

"Then I wouldn't be helping," she replied. *Then I'd be stuck with my broken heart and itchy texting finger.*

"Place needs a vacuum."

"No, it doesn't. That house is spotless and sparse. Even the windows are smudge-free."

Asher ignored her, clicked his tongue and Dare started to walk again. Hula-Hoop knew to follow, so she did.

"How often do you ride the fence looking for holes?" she asked, moving Hula-Hoop up so that she was riding beside Asher.

"Few times a week. There are trees around that can fall and knock down the fence. Wolves and foxes can get caught in the fence. And we've found Fumble out here tangled in the wire before, too."

"What is with that goat?" she asked. "Does he have a death wish?"

"He's just an idiot."

"Whoever named him was spot-on."

"That was me."

She grinned at him. "Well, you chose well."

They rode in silence for a while until Asher stopped Dare and lifted his chin in the direction of the fence.

Her eyes went buggy. "What the—" Someone had not only cut the fence wire, but there were vehicle tracks in the snow along the outside of the fence, then they turned into the field through the hole. Even she could see that whoever had done this had had the proper tools with them to cut the wire. The snow covered the tracks quite well, but they were still noticeable. "Who would do this?"

He slid off Dare and grabbed the coil of extra wire that he brought with him. "There are some locals who are fuck-nut hillbillies. They like to come and do donuts in the field. In the winter they bring their snowmobiles, the rest of the time its their ATVs or four-bys. Haven't been by in a while. It's why we ride the fence, if we send the horses or goats out into the field and there are holes like these, they could escape or be stolen."

"But I don't understand the point of the donuts."

He glanced at her as he walked backward to re-wire the fence. "I don't understand most people, but I don't waste my energy trying to figure them out."

He didn't need to ask her for her to see that the job would be faster and easier with two people, so she slid off Hula-Hoop and helped him fix the fence.

"Thanks," he said once they'd climbed back onto their horses.

"You're welcome."

He grunted. "We need to get back, can't be out here when it gets dark. It's not safe."

They rode again in silence, only this time, Triss didn't mind. The wind was wicked and her face was going numb, so she just kept her head down as they continued to ride along the fence line. She wasn't even watching where they were going, she just trusted Hula-Hoop to follow Dare. So when they turned the corner and the wind was suddenly at their backs, it was like she'd just stepped out of a tunnel and into the light.

There were no other holes in the fence that needed to be repaired. They spotted wolf fur on some of the wire and some faint wolf tracks, but nothing more. Asher did plan to go double-check his chicken numbers after seeing the wolf prints, though. He said that the snow made animals get hungry, and hunger made them take risks.

When he said *risks,* he glanced at her. "Was that why you jumped into the corral with Mercy? You were hungry?" His snort of mirth caught her off guard and rather than scowl at him for bringing up something she thought they'd put to rest, she shook her head and smiled.

"That's exactly why. I was starved and delirious. Couldn't think straight."

"That's what I figured," he murmured as they climbed off their horses and led them into the barn.

They took off the saddles, brushed down the horses, and like she promised, Triss made sure she gave Hula-Hoop a few extra carrots and some snuggles and ear scratches as a thank you for braving the snow with her. That attention, of course, was noticed by Macklin, who brayed and snorted until Triss went over and showed him some love, too.

"I have no time to wallow when I'm up to my eyeballs with making sure you're getting the attention you need, huh, Macklin?" she said, pressing a kiss to the bridge of his nose. "Who needs dumb boyfriends when I can spend Christmas with you?"

Macklin lifted his nose and nudged her, which was his way of saying "More ear scratches." She obliged, of course, because how could she not when the man asking for ear scratches was just that handsome?

Chapter Seven

No chickens were missing, thankfully. But as he re-entered the barn, after visiting the henhouse, Asher stopped just before he came into view of Triss and Macklin.

She was talking to the old horse, which wasn't anything to give him pause. He spoke more to his horses than he did anybody else. And he preferred their conversation to anyone else's, as well. It was *what* she was telling Macklin that made him duck behind the tack room and listen.

Hannah had mentioned that Triss had just been dumped by her boyfriend, but she hadn't gone into any greater detail than that. He'd just assumed that it'd been a relationship that was maybe six months old and the guy ended things before he had to buy a Christmas or Valentine's Day present.

A shitty move for any guy to do, but Asher knew guys who did it. They dated women between February and November, then got out of dodge just after Thanksgiving until February 15th, only to start the whole sick cycle again.

Because you know, buying women gifts was the absolute worst thing in the world.

More often than not he hated men. And all the time he hated people in general.

Horses were so much better in every single way.

Nate had taken their dog, Bruno, with him for the company on the drive and Asher sorely missed the Aussie Shepard with the different colored eyes. He wouldn't be letting Nate take their dog again, that was for sure.

"What's wrong with me, Macklin?" Triss whispered. "I thought things with Lorne and I were on the right track. That by this time next year we'd be engaged and planning to get married. What does *Echo* have that I don't?"

Echo?

He'd boarded a horse named Echo on the ranch for a while. A nippy mare with a big ego if he was being completely honest. Not his favorite horse, but other than Mercy, he rarely hated any horse. Mercy was just a dick, though.

But more importantly, there was a person named Echo?

Or did Triss's boyfriend leave her for a horse?

He'd heard rumors that Catherine the Great had orchestrated a pulley system so she could have sex with a horse, but he didn't believe it. And he really doubted that it'd be as fulfilling in reverse for a guy to fuck a horse.

No, her stupid boyfriend left her for a human named Echo.

Dear God, what was this world coming to? Would he hear of a person named Hula-Hoop soon, too?

"And you want to know the worst part about it all, Macklin?" She sniffed. "I'm crying more over the fact that Lorne leaving me just makes me feel like I'll never find that person, find that soul-shattering love. Not that I lost Lorne. How horrible is that? I'm not upset about losing *him*, just how losing him makes me feel. Because why would I want somebody who dumps their girlfriend they just moved in with for their old culinary school girlfriend, then get pissed off when I took my own Instant Pot with me? It was my Instant Pot, Macklin. Mine. Why would I leave that for Lorne and Echo to use?"

What was an Instant Pot?

Macklin made a nose in his throat. Her sniffles grew louder.

"You've been a really great distraction, Macklin, thank you. Otherwise, I'd be texting Lorne all the mean, immature things that I want to say but shouldn't."

Asher's lip twitched upward.

What kinds of things was she too mature to say?

"Like how his last alfredo sauce tasted burnt to me, and that I make better bread than he does. You don't know the man, Macklin, but he's a bread *snob* and would take that insult like I'd just called his mama fat or something."

Asher stifled a chuckle. He liked her fire.

He'd never ask her, but he'd been burning with curiosity to know what Hannah had said to her after asking to be taken off speakerphone. Whatever it was, it'd turned Triss's face to the color of a cherry blossom in April and made her yell into the phone more than once.

If he were to guess, his not-so-subtle niece was telling Triss she should *hump* Asher, just like she'd texted Asher again today telling him to *hump* Triss.

He didn't dare text her back and say he'd been thinking of little else since she knocked on his door.

Her murmurs with Macklin were quieter now and he couldn't hear them, so wanting to make sure that he announced his presence and gave her time to compose herself, he counted to fifty in his head, then opened the side door and loudly closed it again. "All the chickens are there," he announced, louder than necessary.

She'd jumped when he slammed the door and he caught her wiping her hands beneath her eyes. But there was no hiding the fact that she'd been crying. Her brown eyes were red-rimmed and watery, but most of all, they were sad.

He cleared his throat. "It's getting dark."

Should he acknowledge the fact that she'd been crying? Was that the right thing to do? Or was it better if he acted normal and pretended that he didn't notice her puffy eyes or the fact that she was sniffling? Allow her to save face.

He had no idea how to handle a crying woman, never had. It was why his relationships didn't last much longer than a few weeks. When women got sticky and emotional, he ended things. It was just easier. He was emotionally unavailable, and they needed to learn that sooner rather than later. He'd never be the man they wanted or needed him to be, and there was no changing him, either.

"What do we have to do now?" she asked, kissing Macklin's nose.

"Feed them again, make sure their water troughs are full, but I can do that if you want to head inside."

She shook her head and sniffed again. "Nope. Put me to work."

After overhearing her, he realized now that she needed the distraction. If she went into the house alone, she'd text Lorne the Thorne and regret it. If she kept her mind distracted and her fingers busy, she wouldn't be able to dwell or text.

Nodding, he jerked his head to the hose hanging on the wall. "You're on water duty."

Grinning through the sadness, she nodded. "Can do, boss."

He let her help him as much as he could, but eventually, there was nothing left for her to do, so he sent her into the house and finished up what he needed to do in the barn alone. Normally, he and Nate and whatever other ranch hands they had with them worked in silence. Everyone knew their jobs and what needed to be done. They didn't require many directions. Triss however, needed a bit of tutelage, but she was also a fast learner, she hadn't been lying when she said that.

He caught her chatting with Mercy when she went to fill his water. The black beast hung his massive head over the side of his stall and let her pet him. But when Asher came near, the horse's head started to thrash and he made a big fuss.

What was his fucking problem?

No horse had ever reacted to Asher like that before. It was all he could do to get Mercy out and back into his stall earlier that day, and he was not looking forward to doing it again tomorrow.

He hadn't noticed any of the ranch hands having such a hard time with the horse, either. Was it just Asher, Mercy didn't like?

By the time he entered the house, stomping the snow off his boots before he went inside, it was pitch black outside and had started to snow heavily again. The wind was still blowing and he was worried his nose was going to freeze the fuck off in the short walk from the barn to the house.

The smell of roast vegetables and chicken filled his nostrils the second he stepped inside. She was cooking?

The fire in the wood stove was also roaring. Had she stoked the stove, too?

Tinkering sounds in the kitchen prompted him to walk through the house with his coat still on toward the humming woman standing over the sink. She'd ditched the knit cap he gave her and had also apparently had a shower. Her hair was back up in one of those messy bun things on her head, and she had those hip-grazing pajama pants on and a black tank top.

"You cooked?" he asked, immediately cringing inwardly at such a stupid, rhetorical question.

She jumped a little at his voice, having obviously not heard him come in, what with the music she had playing from her phone. Spinning around, and bringing soapy bubbles with her from the sink, she smiled hopeful at him. "I did. Still trying to earn my keep, you know? I found some beer in the fridge, so I hope you don't mind that I used one to roast the chicken."

He blinked.

"It won't be ready for another half hour, so if you want to run and shower and warm-up you have time." Her smile was closed-lipped this time and flatter.

He stood there for another moment, then with a nod and a grunt, he hung up his coat and headed upstairs to go shower—just like he'd been told to do.

And fuck if he didn't beat off in the shower to the image of Triss standing there all cute and sexy in her tank top, PJs and messy bun.

He was probably a giant asshole not saying anything to her except the idiotic and rhetorical "*You cooked?*" but he was just too stunned to say anything else. And not stunned to find her in the kitchen cooking, because she'd made lunch and had mentioned her beer can chicken. It was how good it made him feel inside to come into the house after a long day in the field and barn and find her there waiting for him.

And that feeling shocked the shit out of him.

The fact that he liked having her there, liked how he felt having her in his house, in his kitchen was terrifying, but in an oddly satisfying way.

And no, it wasn't because she was cooking for him and he wanted a woman in the kitchen and blah, blah, blah feminist rant here. He didn't give a crap about whether she could cook or not. It was that she was there waiting for him. For him.

He knew she had a job, a career and he would never expect her or any woman with a career to quit their job and become a housewife. He also didn't begrudge those women who became "domestic goddesses" as his mother had called herself, and tended to the home and children.

If men were free to do whatever they wanted, women should be, too.

And the fact that she was a speech pathologist spoke to him, too. He'd had a slight stutter as a kid and a speech pathologist had really helped him overcome his anxieties and conquer his stutter.

Dressed in gray sweatpants and a white T-shirt he went downstairs, not bothering with socks. The smell of roast chicken and veggies was even stronger now and his stomach rumbled in anticipation of what was to come.

"Perfect timing," she sang, turning around with a large platter heaped with chicken and veggies. She'd set the table, and had apparently found a bottle of red wine and poured them each a glass. She caught him staring at the wine glasses and her cheeks bloomed with color. "I hope you don't mind that I poured that wine. It wasn't for a special occasion was it?"

He shook his head. "No. It's fine."

Relief flickered in her eyes and she smiled. "Well, have a seat. I hope you're hungry."

He was starving.

She set the platter in the center of the table and took the seat she'd used that morning and afternoon which was next to where he sat at the head of the table. "Dig in."

He did as instructed, loading his plate with the roasted broccoli, potatoes, carrots and chicken. She'd even made a gravy.

With hope in her eyes, she watched as he took the first few bites. Nibbling on the inside of her lip, her gaze followed his fork from the plate to his mouth.

"How is it?" she asked.

He swallowed and pinned his gaze on her. "It's delicious, thank you."

Her chest heaved on a sigh. "Oh good. Even when I thought the food was delicious, Lorne always had something to complain about with my cooking. Too much salt, not enough salt. You should have added a dash of smoked paprika if you wanted to elevate this from plain to extraordinary." That bit about her ex was murmured almost under her breath and most definitely was intended just for herself.

"Well, Lorne sounds like a fucking douche who doesn't know what he's talking about. This is amazing. Thank you, Triss." He offered her a grim smile before taking a sip of his wine.

She beamed and it damn near took his breath away.

"Thank you, Asher. That means a lot."

Silence thudded through the kitchen and his heart thumped wildly as its softest parts tried to recover from the unwitting admission he'd just made to her. It shouldn't be such a big deal to compliment someone on their food, and yet he knew that what he said carried more weight with Triss than it would the average person. The way she was looking at him beneath her lashes said as much and he had to keep his pulse from racing and his hands from reaching out, throwing her down on the table and taking her mouth like he owned it.

The platter of chicken and vegetables was nearly empty, so were their wine glasses by the time Asher stood up from the table and began to clear dishes. "Thank you," he said, his back to her as he opened the dishwasher.

"Thank you for letting me stay here. I will reimburse you for the meals, I promise."

He shook his head and grunted. "Don't. You're a guest and you're helping out a lot here. We're square."

And even if she wasn't helping him in the barn, or cooking for him, he'd never dream of charging her for meals or her room. He wasn't hard up for cash by any stretch and that wasn't the right thing to do.

He should have heard her sidle up beside him, he was trained to hear things better than most, but she appeared at his side almost like an apparition and he sucked in a sharp breath, which only made him inhale her sweet, floral scent.

"Same thing tomorrow?" she asked.

He nodded and took a half-step away from her, before he was muddled any further by her smell and heat. "Everyday."

"Well, I'm game."

They cleaned up the dishes in quiet, and for a man who preferred quiet to unnecessary chatter, he found he actually missed her need for conversation. However, not enough to instigate any of his own.

"Good night," she said hanging up the dish towel and pouring a second glass of wine.

He searched her face for a reason or an opening to keep her from retreating to her room for the night. But he didn't see one and couldn't think of anything engaging or worthwhile to say, so like an idiot, he nodded and said, "Good night."

She disappeared down the hallway and he waited for the door of her room to *snick* shut before he exhaled and scrubbed his hand down his face. He needed to get a hold of himself. She was hurting, and just because Hannah had given him permission to *hump* her friend, did not mean he was going to, or that Triss was interested in him that way.

A couple of years ago, Nate had convinced him to buy a hot tub. Asher had been dead-set against it, but Nate said it would help soothe their aching muscles after a hard day of ranching. He hadn't been wrong.

Now, Asher was out in the tub almost every night with a lowball of whiskey and a joint letting the jets pummel his back and shoulders until every last knot was untangled.

Pouring himself a double, and grabbing his tin of premium pre-rolled kush, he headed to the laundry room off the kitchen. He stripped down to nothing, wrapped a towel around his waist, slid his feet into sandals, and headed out to go and try to fucking relax.

But the way his cock was standing at attention as he thought about what it'd be like to fuck Triss in the hot tub told him he'd probably need to smoke two joints to even remotely chill the fuck out. And even then, he knew it wasn't guaranteed.

Chapter Eight

With her wine glass empty, Triss carefully opened the door of her room while clutching her tablet under her arm, and scuffed her slippered feet into the kitchen.

The house was dark, except for the orange glow of the fire in the wood stove.

Her sisters, Pasha and Rayma had texted her that they were together and wanted to video chat. So Triss told them she would just grab more wine then call them.

Once her wine glass was full, she decided to sit in the chair closest to the fire rather than return to her room. She could be quiet and not disturb the slumbering sexy enigma upstairs while chatting with her sisters. Well, she might need to tell Rayma to keep her voice down, but Pasha had little kids, she knew how to be quiet.

It was just that Triss's room was so boring and she wasn't tired, even though she should be given how early she woke up and how much physical labor she'd done that day. But her brain couldn't turn off.

And no way was she in the mood to read one of the many romance novels Pasha kept suggesting she read. Why read about couples getting their happily ever after when Triss was sitting there trying to reassemble the pieces of her shattered heart with Elmer's glue and it just wasn't holding.

Pulling a knit blanket over her legs, she called her sisters and after four rings the video engaged and up popped their beautiful faces.

"Hey sexy lady," Rayma cooed.

"Hi," Triss said, forcing a smile.

Pasha made a pouty face. "You look sad. What's wrong?"

Sipping her wine, Triss heaved a sigh that made her shoulders slump. "Lorne dumped me."

"He what?" Rayma screamed, loud enough that Triss winced and pulled the tablet away from her face.

"Volume," Pasha reprimanded with an eye roll.

"He what?" Rayma repeated this time with an exaggerated whisper.

"He dumped me," Triss said again. "Reconnected with his culinary school girlfriend—Echo—and realized they're souffle mates. He's moving her in to our apartment."

"But you're on the lease," Rayma protested. "He can't do that."

"It's not worth fighting him over. I don't like the place enough to make it a battle. I've packaged up all of my things and they're being put into storage by a friend of Hannah's who owns a moving company. I'll deal with it all and find a place to live when I get back. If I have to live in an Airbnb for a month, then so be it." The fight had pretty much gone out of her the moment Lorne *told* her she needed to move out. Yes, she could have put up a stink and taken it to the landlord, but did she really want to have any more necessary dealings with an asshole like Lorne than was necessary? If he treated her so poorly after three years of dating, she just needed to be done with him and cut her losses.

Her heart still hurt like a fresh burn despite that revelation, though, there was no escaping it.

"You're spending Christmas with Hannah, then?" Pasha asked.

"Was supposed to, but her flight from Manhattan was rerouted to Oklahoma because of snow, then she slipped on black ice and broke her ankle and hip. So now she's in the hospital."

Rayma's button nose wrinkled. "In Oklahoma?"

"Yep."

"And you're where?" Pasha, always the serious one, and a total *mom* was full of concern with zero patience for superfluous details. "Who are you with? Are you okay?"

"I'm in Colorado, outside of Denver at Hannah's uncles' ranch."

"Why?" her sisters said at the same time.

"Because this was where Hannah and I were going to spend Christmas and I arrived and she didn't and now I'm stuck here because of the snow."

"With who?" Rayma asked, her brown eyes squinting. All five of the Young sisters looked a lot alike. Same caramel-brown hair, same gold-flecked brown eyes and naturally tanned skin. But of all of them, Rayma and Pasha looked the most similar, particularly since they both chose to have thick highlights of dark blonde in their hair and styled it the same way, too.

"How are the kids?" Triss asked.

"They're fine," Pasha responded deadpanned. "Who are you at this ranch with? Should we be worried? I'll call the Denver police and have them drive out there for a wellness check."

Just then a door behind Triss opened, sending a gust of icy air careening through the house.

A shiver wracked her body involuntarily and she tugged the blanket around her tighter as she craned her neck around just in time to see a surprised-looking Asher, wearing nothing but a low-slung towel on his hips, walk out from the laundry room.

"Holy fuck, who is that?" Rayma demanded. "Man's like a goddamn ice cream cone I wanna lick until he melts all over my face."

"Rayma," Pasha scolded, "he can hear you!"

"Sorry," Asher murmured. "Was in the hot tub, didn't know you were out here."

Her mouth was dry and her eyes wide as she tracked him across the house to the stairs where he disappeared into the dark.

"Be still my pulsating clitoris," Rayma purred, when Triss finally lifted the tablet up again to face her sisters who were both grinning like two Cheshire cats.

"Shut it," Triss warned.

"I'm gonna say you're fine, no need to call the cops, and you are getting over that breakup by getting under a cowboy," Pasha said, unable to stop smiling.

"He's a *rancher* not a cowboy, and no. I'm not *under* him."

"Oh, so you're doing the cowgirl thing then, huh?" Rayma teased. "Riding that stallion straight to the races."

"Oh my God, shut the fuck up right now, you brat." Her face was on fire. "Nobody is riding anybody anywhere. I'm not on top, under, in front of or any other sexual configuration you two wanton beasts can come up with. Leave it alone."

"Why the fuck not?" Rayma asked, bewildered. "If I didn't have a sexy piece of ass waiting for me at home to go mount, I'd be all over that. And since you *don't* have a sexy piece of ass waiting for you at home, you should definitely go and mount that Mustang. Ride him bareback or reverse. Climb up on that beast and chafe your inner thighs."

"I'm hanging up now," Triss said with a hiss.

"Okay, okay, we'll stop," Pasha said, swatting Rayma on the arm. "But in all seriousness, who is he?"

"Hannah's Uncle Asher. Apparently, her dad was from her grandfather's first marriage, and Asher and his brother are from their dad's second marriage, hence the big age gap and why he's closer to Hannah's age than her dad's."

"There are two of them?" Rayma squealed. "Tell me you're the cheese in the middle of this cowboy Christmas sandwich. Please!"

"Rancher, not cowboy. And no. Nate is in Texas delivering a yearling, and then he's going to Oklahoma to pick up Hannah. Get your pea brain out of the gutter."

Rayma just grinned. "It has its own address in the gutter, get over it."

"So it's just you and this Asher guy at the ranch?" Pasha asked.

Triss nodded. "Yep. And the horses, goats, pony, chickens and miniature horses."

"Is he gay? Married? Widowed?" Rayma probed. "Why hasn't he tried to mount you like a mare in heat?"

"I'm seriously going to hang up if you do not shut this child up," Triss said, addressing Pasha.

Pasha murmured something to Rayma, which made their baby sister pout then disappear from the screen. Then it was just Pasha and Triss. "She's gone," Pasha said, her brown eyes turning soft. "How are you really, though. I'm sorry Lorne dumped you. That sucks. But if I'm being honest, the guy was a bit of a douche. Just don't throw that in my face if you get back together, okay?"

"We won't be getting back together, trust me. So yeah, say what you want about him. Don't hold back."

"Does that apply to me, too?" Rayma shouted.

"No!" Triss replied, though the pull of her lip into a half-smile wasn't unwelcomed. For all her lack-of-a-filter faults, Rayma had really come into her own in the last few years. She was a hardworking, brilliant, kind-hearted soul who would defend those she loved with everything she had.

"I'll text you my list of his faults," Rayma replied. "Maybe buy more data to receive the file."

Triss rolled her eyes and focused on her older sister. "As awkward as it was—and still is in some ways—being here had been good for me. I'm so busy helping Asher with the animals that I don't have a lot of time to wallow and dwell." She laughed in spite of herself. "I mean, I still am wallowing and dwelling, but I'm not doing as much of it as I could."

Pasha pressed her lips together in a flat line. "I wish I could hug you right now. You look like you need a hug."

"I'm hugging horses. Hannah promised me goat cuddles, but so far none of them are snugglers. But there's one old horse here who Asher says would literally climb into my lap if he could. So I go cuddle and talk to Macklin when I'm sad."

"How much longer do you think you'll be there?"

Shrugging, Triss balanced the tablet on her knees and reached for her wine. "A couple of days I think. Snow hasn't let up and I kind of want to wait to see how Hannah is doing. But we'll see. I don't want to overstay my welcome since I pretty much wasn't welcome in the first place. I just showed up on his doorstep in the middle of the night."

"What? Hannah didn't tell them you were coming?"

"Hannah is being Hannah and keeps telling me to hump her uncle."

Pasha snorted. "I mean ... the man is fine. I'm going to have to agree with Hannah on this one."

"I third that opinion," Rayma chimed in.

"I'm just appreciative of the distraction and that being here is keeping my mind off my problems back home and my hands too busy to text Lorne what I *really* thought of his ossa bucco."

"Already on it," Rayma called. "I said in a Yelp review that his mole gave me food poisoning and his pico de gallo was uninspired, derivative and yucky."

Triss buried her face in her hand. "Oh my God."

"She's trying to help," Pasha said with a chuckle.

"I just hope she's at least using an untraceable username and those reviews aren't going to somehow make their way back to me."

"I'm also leaving reviews about Echo and the restaurant she's at," Rayma added gleefully, her face still not on screen, but her personality coming at Triss in giant waves. "Does diarrhea have two *r*'s or one? *Tasted like diarrhea in my mouth. Do not recommend.*"

"You need to stop," Triss said, sipping her wine. "Like seriously."

"I'll call the health authority in your town in the morning. Say Lorne's food held definite notes of rat poisoning. Do you think rat poisoning is bitter or more umami?"

"You're welcome to take the high road, sis," Pasha said. "But that doesn't mean we have to. We have your back one thousand percent." As if she needed a reminder of that, the tattoo on her hip tingled. All five of the Young sisters had gone and gotten identical tattoos last summer. It was five interlocking hearts in a row, each one slightly smaller than the one before it. The hearts were not colored in, except for the heart which corresponded to that sister's birth order. So the second heart in the chain on Triss was a soft lilac-purple color, since she was the second oldest at thirty-four.

"I've also set up a Craigslist ad for a free couch and put Lorne's number down as the contact," Rayma said. "Fun times for that douchebag."

Triss cringed, but the smile that tugged at her lips was one she couldn't fight any longer. She loved her sisters so much, they knew just how to cheer her up.

"Now, go climb into bed with that sexy cowboy and forget all about Lorne the shitty chef," Pasha said, waggling her eyebrows playfully. "Were those dog tags hanging around his neck?"

Triss nodded.

Pasha crooned. "Oh you know how I like my military men. Their attention to detail and desire to *succeed* in bed is unprecedented."

"Can confirm," Heath, Pasha's husband called out from somewhere in the background. Heath was a retired special operative himself and now he and his three brothers ran a security and surveillance company. "They don't call me the *Big Eater* for nothing."

Triss cringed.

Pasha just grinned. "I want to hear that your Christmas was spent getting cuddled by horses and railed by a cowboy. Capiche?"

All she did was groan, smile and roll her eyes.

"That's an order. I'm the big sister and I'm *telling* you to save the horse and ride a cowboy."

"Rancher," Triss corrected, draining her wine glass.

"Fine, then save a horse and ride that rancher." She blew Triss a kiss, Rayma appeared back on the screen, they all said how much they loved each other, sent best wishes for Christmas, and said goodbye.

When she went to put her wine glass in the sink, Triss was grinning ear-to-ear and it wasn't just because she was tipsy from the wine. It was because no matter how bad things got, or how broken her heart might be, she knew there were still people out there who loved her, who had her back and who wanted her to be happy. And those people were her sisters and she was really freaking lucky to have them.

Chapter Nine

Okay, he knew he hung out on the top step eavesdropping on Triss and her sister's video chat way too long, but after hearing that one sister react to seeing him, how could he not?

And then it was nearly impossible to keep himself from laughing as Triss attempted to keep her sisters in line, but ultimately failed.

One thing was for sure, though, he could hear the love they had for each other in their voices.

It was good that Triss had people in her corner like that, even if they were thousands of miles away.

Asher had people like that, too. His brother Nate, and his brothers in arms, as well. Aaron Steele, Colton Hastings, Rob Cahill, Barnes Wark, Ryker and Decker McKnight, and Pete Callaghan. They'd all seen each other at their absolute worst and still no matter what they had each other's backs.

Besides Nate, he hadn't seen the others in ages, but he knew if he needed something they'd be there in a flash. Aaron, Colton and Rob all had wives and families now. Barnes was married, too. But they had a group text going on and updated each other every now and then. He knew that Ryke, Cal and Deck were still working often going undercover for months on end. They'd send a picture of a remote location, some beach or a barren desert to let the rest of them know where they were. The guys with kids sent baby pictures, and Barnes who didn't have kids with his wife—and didn't want them—would send pictures of the latest piece of furniture he'd built captioning it, "my baby 114.7 lbs 93inches long." At least this was what he'd done for the last pic of a dresser he'd sent everyone.

Asher showered again, just to rinse off the hot tub chemicals before he climbed into bed. So Hannah had told Triss to *hump* him. He kind of thought she might have.

And Triss's sisters both supported the idea.

But Triss didn't give any inclination as to whether she supported the idea, too. He'd stuck around long enough to see if she said anything along that line, but she hadn't.

Which meant, she wasn't interested.

That sucked, but he'd deal with it.

She was hurting, he had to keep reminding himself of that. Her head was all fucked up from the breakup, so the last thing she needed was for him to come in and confuse her even further, particularly since she was probably looking for a happily ever after, and he was just not that kind of guy.

As he lay in bed, he brought up the barn cam on his phone and checked the videos. He had a camera pointed at each stall so that if a horse went into labor or was sick, he could check the video feed first.

Everybody was tucked in snug for the night, and he was about to put his phone on his nightstand and turn in, too, when something made him go back to the feed for Carolina's stall.

That was his mare that was due any day. He'd checked on her several times throughout the day and she showed no real imminent signs of being in labor. Mind you, this was her first pregnancy and every horse was different. Yes, she was engorged where was to be expected and was showing signs that she was getting close, but she hadn't been agitated or colicky like his other mares when they were

WHITLEY COX

ready to foal.

He'd also tested the calcium in her mammary secretions right before coming in for dinner using a test strip and there was no increase in calcium. An increase usually meant imminent foaling.

But she was imminent now. Her belly quivered and she was making labor noises. Her tail was lifting and he watched her flop to the ground and roll, getting the foal into position.

He and Nate had moved her to the larger stall a few weeks ago where she'd have plenty of room to foal laying down if she chose to. If a mare foaled in the spring, summer or fall, they liked to allow them to do it in the pasture if they could, but Carolina had gone into heat in early February, so they knew they'd have a winter foal and she wouldn't want to give birth in the snow.

She stood up abruptly and started to nip at her own flanks and ankles.

Fuck, she was foaling. She was close. He needed to get out there and help her. Muck her stall, lay down fresh wheat straw, clean her up so she was ready for the birth.

No rest for the wicked, or a rancher.

Swinging his legs over the side of the bed, he got dressed quick and was down the stairs and shoving his feet into his boots and arms into his coat in no time.

He ran across the driveway, through the snow toward the barn, and headed inside, flicking on lights as he went.

Carolina made a typical horse-in-labor noise from her stall near the end of the barn.

He'd helped many a mare foal over the years, both on his own ranch and on his uncle's, but he always had a vet on standby if shit went sideways. But it was December twenty-second and snowing like the goddamn North Pole, no way would his vet, or any vet be willing to come out tonight.

He just had to pray that Carolina had an easy delivery and nothing wrong went down.

She really should be sleeping.

Even though it wasn't past midnight, she would want to be up with Asher tomorrow to help him with the animals, so she needed her rest.

But her brain just would not shut off.

And it wasn't thoughts of Lorne that kept her awake. It was thoughts of Asher and what was hidden beneath that towel that had her hot and bothered and unable to close her eyes without picturing him nearly naked and wet.

And the fact that he had a giant tattoo on his back of angel wings just made her want to run her tongue across that ink and have him take her to heaven.

She was contemplating pushing her fingers down her panties just to ease the ache in her lower belly and help her sleep when the thunderous steps of Asher running down the stairs had her bolting upright in bed. She heard him fumbling at the foyer, then he threw the front door open and ran out, letting it slam behind him.

She was out of bed and at the living room window in five seconds, but he had already vanished. It didn't take much guessing to figure out where he went, though, since lights in the barn began to flick on.

Was something wrong with one of the horses?

That's when she remembered that two of the horses were pregnant.

Running back to her room, she tossed on the same pair of jeans that she'd worn all day, and her dark gray hoodie over her black pajama tank top. She didn't bother with a bra and barely remembered socks before she was shoving her feet into her boots, tugging her coat over her arms, and taking off into the darkness toward the barn.

Sounds a horse heavily breathing greeted her as she stepped into the bright, warm barn.

With just a quick three-second pause at Macklin's stall to touch his cheek, she kept walking down toward the end where the ready to foal mare had been earlier today.

She slowed her pace, not wanting to spook either Asher or the horse, and stepped quietly up to the front of the stall.

He was crouched next to Carolina who was breathing heavily, and rubbing her neck. "You got this, baby girl," he cooed. "You can do this."

Carolina, a beautiful light brown horse with a white forehead and nose, and blonde hair lifted her head and glanced up at Triss, which caused Asher to do the same.

"How can I help?" she asked, peeling off her hoodie and draping it over the stall before stepping in next to Asher and crouching down.

"Stay with her. I need to get fresh straw and clean out this stall a bit. We'll need to wash her vulva and teats, too. But for now, just let her know she's not alone."

Triss nodded and inched forward, claiming Asher's spot next to Carolina and petting the horse's neck while he stepped out of the stall.

"It'll all be over soon, sweetheart," Triss cooed, petting the panting horse. "You got this. This time tomorrow you'll have a bouncy baby to cuddle. How exciting is that?"

Carolina rolled around a bit, so Triss moved back to give her some room. The horse made a bunch of farting noises and it looked like she was peeing. Then a weird white balloon thing emerged from her behind.

"Uhhh ... Asher," Triss called, her voice shaky with panic. "Is that balloon thing normal?"

He appeared in the doorway of the stall a moment later, fresh straw in his arms. "Yes. It's fine. That's the allantoic membrane. And if looked like she peed, that is just placental fluid. All normal. All okay." He reached outside the stall and grabbed a shovel, handing it to her. "Can you help me clear the manure? Just toss it into the wheelbarrow there."

Nodding, Triss did as she was told and in no time, they had the stall cleaned out with a fresh layer of straw.

Asher disappeared, so Triss went back to comforting Carolina who tossed and turned, her nostrils flaring wildly as she breathed through the contractions.

He appeared again with a bucket of steaming water and a few bubbles. With a soft sponge, he gently wiped the horse's swollen nipples, then her behind. Using green painter's tape, before Triss had even shown up, Asher had taped Carolina's tail to the top of her rump, probably so she didn't get it soiled during the birth.

"Shouldn't be much longer," he said, tucking the bucket to the outside of the stall.

Triss rubbed Carolina's neck. "You're doing great, sweetie." The white balloon-like thing had grown in size and Carolina alternated between standing up and laying down, flopping onto her side and groaning lightly.

Another rush of liquid had Triss's eyes going wide. The balloon popped and what happened next was something she would never ever forget.

Two little hooves poked out and then a nose, a head, a neck, legs, a body and finally two more legs, and then the foal was out. Carolina immediately stood up and the foal, which appeared to be a little girl, damp and beautifully brown with a blonde mane like her mother, wobbled and fell three times before finally finding her balance and seeking out her mother for milk.

"Thank fuck," Asher breathed, patting Carolina on the neck, then kissing her. "I was worried the baby would be breach or upside down."

A sheen of tears made Triss's eyes blurry as she took in the beauty of what she'd just watched. The miracle of life.

Asher bent down to check how the foal was nursing, patting the little girl on the back before standing back up and moving around to stand behind Carolina. "We need her to expel the placenta."

"How does that happen?"

"By baby nursing a lot to get her uterus to contract and expel it. Otherwise, I'll have to give her a shot of Pitocin, which will piss her right off because the cramping is insane."

Triss's face fell. "Oh, let's hope it doesn't come to that." She went to Carolina and pressed her head to the horse's forehead. "Come on, sweet Carolina, you don't need drugs, you got this. You delivered that perfect little girl all on your own, you can do this, too."

Carolina shuffled a bit and made a noise.

When the foal broke away from nursing, Asher took that as an opportunity to give her a check over. Triss sunk to her knees and watched in fascination as the little foal, so perfect, who just moment ago had been inside her mother, was now walking around in the world. More tears veiled her vision and Asher glanced at her. "You okay?"

"This is just the best possible Christmas present I ever could have wished for. She's perfect, isn't she?" Worry edged her tone. What if there was something wrong with the foal?

"She is," he confirmed. "Would you like to name her?"

Triss sucked in a breath. "Me?"

He shrugged. "Why not?"

"I ... how do you name a horse?"

"Same way you name a human, just with a bit more license for creativity. I'm okay with a horse name Hula-Hoop, but if a kid comes to our ranch camp in the summer with that name, I'm calling child protective services." He cracked a half-smile that took him from handsome to dangerously gorgeous.

The foal trotted over to where they knelt and gently head-butted Asher. "Hmm, little filly. What's your name?"

"Filly ... hmmm. Tilly the Filly?" Triss mused, lifting a brow at him. "It's cute."

He patted the filly on her neck. "Is your name Tilly, little one?" As if to say that calling her by any other name was ridiculous, the foal leaped away in a sort of weird sideways hop and trotted back to her mother.

"Tilly the Filly it is," Asher said with a full-watt smile, turning to face Triss. "I like it."

Triss grinned back at him. "Thank you for allowing me to help. This has been an amazing experience."

"I should have woke you up when I saw she was in labor, but I just ... thought you were sleeping." He scratched at the back of his neck and broke their eye contact, a subtle ruddy color bloomed under his scruff.

"I'm sorry if you heard my sisters react to you coming in from the hot tub. The youngest one has no filter. It's an ongoing issue."

He snorted and that half-smile was back, causing the sleepy butterflies in her belly to wake up and start flying around in a disorganized fashion. "No problem. They ... *she* sounds like a handful."

"More like a bucketful, but yes."

"Listen, you go get some sleep," he said, standing up with a slight groan.

"What are you going to do?"

"I need to stay out here and make sure she passes the placenta. Both mom and foal should be monitored for the first twenty-four hours, so I'll just bring a blanket and stay out here until morning. Done it before, used to it."

She shook her head. "No. I want to stay."

"You don't have to. You're not a rancher, this isn't your job."

"Does it have to be for me to want to help?"

His eyes formed thin slits as he gazed at her thoughtfully, but eventually, he just shrugged. "Okay. I'll go get you a blanket."

She beamed at him, proud of herself for standing her ground and wearing down the big grumpy rancher.

By the time he got back with blankets, and what appeared to be a thermos of tea, Carolina had passed the placenta.

Although she wanted to help, Triss knew better than to step out of place too much, so she didn't touch the placenta or cord. Asher used a shovel to scoop it all up and took it out into the barn to deal with, so she settled into the straw, her butt on the cold, hard ground, and with a blanket over her legs, she leaned her head against the barn wall and closed her eyes.

She didn't expect to fall asleep, given the excitement of the day, but when a warm, soft little body pressed against her thigh and she opened her eyes a crack to find Tilly curled up beside her, Carolina on the other side of her foal, a sense of overwhelming peace washed over Triss and she smiled.

Her life and heart might be in shambles, but this moment right here, was perfect and she was going to hang on to it for as long as she possibly could.

Chapter Ten

Up until that moment, Asher would argue until he was blue in the face that love wasn't in the cards for him or that the concept of love even existed at all.

But coming around the corner and seeing Triss sitting on the floor of the stall with Tilly beside her and Carolina beside Tilly made his heart constrict in his chest and warmth spool through him.

He'd laughed more than once at his "falls in love every Friday night" brother who whole-heartedly believed in love at first sight, soulmates, and fate. Nate was the optimist of the two of them, and despite the fact that they were raised by the same parents and fought the same wars, they could not be more different.

But in the dark depths of his black heart, Asher believed that Triss had shown up on his doorstep for more than just his meddling niece playing matchmaker. She was easy to be around, and although they hadn't talked much, he didn't take her for an idiot. She had bright, intelligent eyes, and she was stubborn but not in a foolish way—well, besides getting into the corral with Mercy. But he couldn't hold that against her forever.

She'd worked so hard yesterday, not complaining about a thing, but just asking what else she could do, and how she could help. And even when he had nothing more for her to do, she found another way to make herself useful by fixing dinner.

He hadn't met a harder working person in a really long time.

Morning hit them hard and fast, or at least it seemed that way, since he didn't feel rested at all. He tended to the animals, fed them, mucked stalls, and made sure Fumble hadn't gnawed through his tether and gone out on a walkabout into the snowy pasture.

He made them the same oatmeal he'd made the morning before, put it in a stumpy thermos along with coffee and cream—with a splash of Irish Cream—in another thermos and brought it to her in the barn.

Her voice had him slowing his pace.

"You are just the most beautiful baby in the whole wide world, yes you are, Miss Tilly. Your mama did such a good job. You should be proud of her. I certainly am." She made a kissing noise. "You did great, Carolina. Birthed a beautiful little girl."

Her giggle warmed him, although even without being able to see her, he could tell there wasn't a lot of heart behind that laugh, besides her love for the horses.

"And you know what else, little Tilly? Your mama loves you so much. She just met you, but she already loves to you the moon and back. Isn't that crazy? To be loved that quickly and that hard by somebody you hardly know?"

A rattled breath was sucked which made the knot forming in this throat threaten to pull tighter.

"I'm not looking for that kind of love. I mean, yeah, I want kids one day that I'll love them like that. But I need somebody to have those kids with first, right? I just want some kind of love." He heard her pat one of the horses. "I guess you're a single mom, aren't you? But you've got a whole ranch helping you raise your baby, and I'm sure little Tilly is going to be sold eventually, so it's not the same." Another rattled breath. "What am I going to do, Tilly? Do I have to live in an Airbnb when I get home? I've been searching for apartments but there's nothing out there that isn't out of my price range or somewhere I'd be afraid of getting stabbed by a gang of rats with tattoos."

Asher had to smother his snort in his elbow. Even sad, she was cracking jokes. It showed her strength and her character. She was sad, possibly even heartbroken, but she wasn't going to let it defeat her.

"Can I just move into your stall with you and your mom, Til? I'll be quiet and clean. All the ear scratches and brushing you can ask for. I can even provide you with first and last month's rent and I have *excellent* references."

Her chuckle was forced again.

"Who am I kidding, Tilly? Your big, grumpy rancher wouldn't let me stay here. Besides, my job is in Connecticut. I'm just here because my friend is a meddler, Mother Nature is angry over global warming and I was desperate to escape the hell that is my world for just a little while. But we all have to face the music eventually, right? You're not going to be able to run around bare-hooved forever. Eventually, they're going to make you wear shoes. Eventually, we all have to wear shoes."

"Is Tilly trying to convince you to let her go bare-hoofed?" He asked, poking his head around the corner. "Don't listen to her. All the foals do it. They woo you with their cuteness but don't let them fool you. They have to wear shoes eventually."

She stroked Tilly's neck. "She can fool me all she wants."

"Here," he handed her the stumpy thermos. "Oatmeal."

She accepted it from him with a small smile. "Thank you."

"And coffee." He set the larger thermos down beside her, before sliding his back along the wall and sinking down to his ass next to her, close enough that their knees touched.

Her heat practically pulsed into him.

"Thank you," she repeated, setting the oatmeal thermos on her lap and opening up the thermos of coffee. She brought it to her nose and inhaled deeply, turning to him with a quirky smile. "Did you spike this?"

He shrugged. "Just don't go stealing my tractor if you get hammered, okay?"

Her smile made him buoyant. "I'm not making any promises. I *do* race

75

tractors back in Connecticut so ... " Her moan after she took a sip had his dick lurching in his jeans, despite his fatigue. "Have you eaten?" she asked, setting the coffee thermos down and unscrewing the oatmeal thermos.

He nodded. "Yeah, so it's all yours."

Her lips twisted. "Ummm ..."

"Problem?"

"Am I supposed to eat it with my hands?"

He hung his head. "Shit. Sorry. Hang on." He went to stand up and run back to the house to grab her a spoon, but her hand on his arm stopped him.

"Wait, it's okay."

His gaze traveled down to where she held on to him, the heat of her hand flowing into him like a hot spring. He lifted his eyes back to her. Flames flickered in the soft brown almost like the gold around her irises was dancing.

He's not sure who moved first or whether time bent and stood still, but the next thing he knew, his mouth was on hers, her hands were in his hair and he was hauling her up to her feet.

They moved like two dancers through the stall and out into the main barn. He guided her, of course, because he knew precisely what he wanted to do, now that they'd snapped the tension-filled air between them.

She let him move her around to the front of the stall, plaster her back against the wall and ravish her mouth. His tongue plunged in and out, savoring the coffee and Irish cream on her lips, loving the way she met him kiss for kiss, bite for bite. Her fingers dove into his hair and tugged, pulling him down to her since there was a significant height difference between them.

When she released his head for a moment, he took that as an opportunity to gather her hands and pin them above her head, holding her in place as he dropped his mouth to her neck and sucked until she gasped and tilted her head to the side so he could have better access.

They didn't speak.

They didn't have to.

Their bodies were saying plenty.

She wanted him and holy fuck did he want her.

She whimpered when he bit her bottom lip, then her hips thrust out against his when he sucked that same lip. She started to grind herself on his thigh and he smiled into their kiss. Yeah, there was no mistaking how much she wanted this.

He grabbed her around the waist and she leaped up onto his hips, her eyes flying open when she realized just how much he wanted this, too. He still had her arms pinned above her head with one of his hands while the other held onto her ass. He kept her against the wall with his hips and she rocked against them, rubbing her heat over his erection and driving him fucking crazy.

With a final plunge of his tongue into her mouth, he growled, tore his lips away, and let her slide down his body, her feet landing on the floor.

Gruffly, he took her hand and lead her over to the saddle stand where his saddle for Dare sat. He placed her hands on the saddle, walked behind her, and toed her legs apart further. "Don't move," he told her, loving the tremble that shook her, and the firm, strong nod that she gave him a second later.

She still had one of those messy top knots in her hair, so that was the first thing to go, he pulled the elastic free, letting her dark caramel waves tumble down her back and over her shoulders.

Sweeping it to one side, he pressed a nip then a kiss to her neck. "Do you want this?" he asked, even though he was like ninety-nine-point-nine percent sure she did.

She nodded.

"I need to hear it," he said, pressing a kiss to her bare shoulder since she was just in a tank top.

"Yes, I want this ... I want you."

He pushed down his groan, grateful that she wasn't looking at him right now.

"I don't have any condoms," he said, continuing to kiss a path down her arm, then back up again, chasing the goosebumps. "But I can assure you I'm clean."

"I got tested the day after Lorne dumped me," she said. "I'm clean, too, and I'm on the pill."

Thank fuck.

Not that he was against just getting her off out here, then waiting until they were in the house to use condoms, but he was really hoping to fuck her out here, too.

While his lips coasted across her shoulder and neck, he reached beneath her and unbuttoned and unzipped her jeans. He kept kissing her as he slid her pants down her slender thighs. When they reached her ankles, he slowly trailed his fingers up the outsides of her thighs, loving every tremble, every shiver that wracked her, because he knew they were out of anticipation, not fear. He bet when he put his hands in her panties they'd be soaked.

When he reached her hips again, he slid his right hand along the waistband across her lower stomach. Slowly, he pushed one, then two fingers down beneath the thin cotton, past the trimmed patch of hair to a slick wet heat.

Just as he suspected, the woman was drenched.

Wiggling his index finger over her clit, he smiled against her shoulder as she sucked in a sharp breath and ground her pelvis down against his hand.

He wanted to taste her. He wanted to taste her so fucking bad.

With his other hand, he pulled her panties down, then removed his fingers from her clit, loving the faint whimper of her protest. He peeled her underwear down to her ankles, letting them meet her jeans, then he crept around behind her, sunk to his knees and flicked out his tongue against her slick, swollen folds.

"Oh God!" she cried out, pushing back against his face.

He grinned and did it again, relishing the sudden gush of her arousal that flowed across his tongue. He drank her down, wiggling his tongue over her clit and enjoying the way her legs wobbled when he flicked the hood.

"Asher ..."

One finger, then another explored her cleft, rubbing and teasing until he finally gave her what he knew she wanted, and that was two fingers deep inside her pussy. Her groan echoed through the barn and she clenched around his fingers.

In and out he pumped, curling his fingers when he was deep inside, hitting that special button, the button that made her knees nearly buckle and her entire body tremble. He had to keep himself from laughing, it was almost a game. If he flicked her clit hood just right with his tongue and pressed up on that spot her knees nearly gave out and her body jerked. He had to keep her from collapsing with his free hand on her back, otherwise, he was sure if he made her come with those moves, her knees really would buckle.

He played her like an instrument, got her singing those sweet notes, then when he knew she was close, he pulled back, removed his fingers, stood up and slapped her left ass cheek hard enough to leave a red print of his hand.

Fuck, yes.

Her yelp of surprise had him pausing, a ribbon of dread wrapping around his throat. Was she not into that?

But the moan that followed that yelp and the way she wiggled that freshly smacked ass at him said she was not only into it, but she liked it and she wanted more.

He grinned and that ribbon of dread untangled from his throat and drifted away.

Preferring to catch her off guard, he counted to five before he smacked the other ass cheek, earning another yelp and moan from the woman bent over his saddle. He didn't wait another five seconds before delivering the third spank to the first cheek. Then he dropped back to his knees, shoved his face between her thighs, his fingers back into her pussy and in less than four seconds she was coming across his tongue, convulsing around his fingers and crying out loud enough to wake the neighbors ten miles away.

When she released the death grip she had on his fingers, he pulled them from her pussy, licked them clean, stood up, dropped his jeans and grabbed her by the hips. "You're sure?" he asked, one more time.

She glanced over her shoulder at him, her eyes bright. But it was her smile that lit up the seemingly perpetual darkness inside of him. Made his heart beat with a sense of newfound purpose and intention, filling him with a joy and desire he couldn't remember feeling before. "Very sure," she said, dragging her top teeth over her bottom lip.

That was all he needed to know. He notched his cock at her dripping center and slowly eased into her tight channel.

"Fuck," he growled.

She pushed back against him. Obviously, he was going too slow for her liking and she wanted all of him and she wanted all of him right now.

Well, he could certainly give her that. Tightening his grip on her hips, he thrust forward until he was fully seated inside her.

Her hissed, "Yesssss," made him lean over her and bite her shoulder.

"You like that?" he asked, scraping his teeth across her soft skin.

"Like it better if you started moving," she replied, squeezing her muscles around him.

His stood up straight and tossed his head back with a laugh. "Oh, Triss, I can move." He smacked her ass once more, which had her tightening around him even harder and him groaning from how fucking good that felt, before he started to pump.

In and out of her heat he pistoned, driving deeper, driving harder, taking her cues and moans of pleasure that she liked what he was doing and wanted more.

He watched as she braced one elbow on the saddle and removed the other hand, pushing it down between her legs to her clit. When she sucked in a breath and tightened around him he groaned.

"Spank me again," she breathed, craning her head around to look at him. "Please."

Holy fuck. Did she even know what she was doing to him? Was she playing? Did she like to play?

Baring his teeth, he raised his right hand and cracked it down hard over her cheek. She exploded around him. He didn't even know she was that close.

Her pussy pulsed and squeezed his cock as if trying to draw him into her body, claim him, consume him.

The heat in his belly intensified, bloomed and as he watched his handprint on her ass grow darker, his balls cinched up and he came, growling and groaning with each pump and pulse of his cock.

For several long seconds, he just stood there. His breathing had returned to normal and his cock began to get soft when he finally stepped away, pulling free of her body. She stood up, too, and went to pull up her panties and jeans, but he stopped her.

"Hold on." He yanked up his own boxers and jeans and walked to the end of the barn where they had a sink. He ran the water until it was warm and folded up some clean paper towels into a thick square, then got it wet with the warm water. "Here," he said returning to her and crouching down, cleaning her up between her legs.

She blinked at him when he stood again. "Um ... thank you."

He nodded.

She pulled up her panties and jeans, tucking her gorgeous hair behind her ear. Her eyes were bright and her lips gorgeously puffy. Tilting her eyes to him, she smiled. "So ..."

"I ..."

"No, let me speak ... please."

He nodded. Was she going to say this was a mistake? Worry blazed an ice-cold trail through him.

"So ... um ... I'm going to eat my oatmeal and drink my coffee, then we're going to do that again. And again. And again. Is that okay?"

All he could do was nod, but his smile nearly broke his damn face.

Chapter Eleven

"This is amazing ..." Triss sighed, settling back against Asher's chest in the hot tub later that night.

They'd done just as she'd said. She finished her oatmeal and coffee, then he took her again in the barn, this time face-to-face and up against the wall before they ran to the house and jumped into his bed. Which was where they stayed for several hours.

But eventually, she needed to shower, they needed to eat and so did the animals.

He said she didn't have to come back out to the barn, but she was already extremely attached to the animals, so of course she'd want to visit Tilly and Carolina. And then of course, Macklin got jealous and started stomping his hoof when he knew she was in the barn and *not* showering him with affection. So she had to give him a solid twenty minutes of scratches and love. Not that she was complaining.

Asher made a sexy rumbly groan sound behind her and offered her the joint between his fingers. "Do you smoke?"

"Haven't in ages," she said, accepting it from him and putting it to her lips. She inhaled deep, held it in her lungs for several long seconds, then released it.

She coughed a few times because her lungs weren't used to the smoke, but the almost instant peace and calm that seeped through her was decadent.

They were naked in the tub and how Asher could be hard again after how many rounds they'd gone that day already was a mystery to her, but not one she cared to uncover. The fact that he could do it was all that mattered.

Wiggling in his lap, she giggled when he growled and nipped her shoulder. "Careful," he said, taking the joint from her and putting it between his lips. "Start something and you'll have to finish it."

"Is that a threat or a promise?"

He passed her back the joint, then grabbed the lowball of whiskey from the deck behind him and sipped. "It's an absolute. You make it hard, it's yours to take care of."

"Have I neglected it so far?" She blew out a cloud of smoke, then put the joint back to her lips for another hit.

"No." His cock twitched beneath her and she laughed. "Just letting you know the rules." He accepted the joint back and took a hit.

Closing her eyes, she settled deeper into his solid frame, his dog tags rested against his chest and brushed against her ear. She reached up with the hand she'd let be in the water and touched them. "I won't pry any further than this, but who did you serve with?"

"Navy," he said gruffly. "Special forces. Nate and I were SEALs."

"Oh. Thank you for answering."

He grunted and his free hand came up from where it'd rested on her thigh and he cupped her breasts, rolling the nipple around between his fingers and making her moan. "You wanna talk about the breakup with that tool?"

"Not really." He didn't seem like the kind of guy who would want to talk about that kind of stuff anyway, so the fact that he asked struck her as strange. But maybe he was trying. She had to give him credit for even bringing it up. The fact that they'd had sex in a dozen positions and he'd spent the better part of the afternoon with his face between her legs, didn't take away from the fact that they hardly knew each other.

He didn't have to be her sounding board.

He grunted again. "You're better off. Guy was an idiot."

She smiled into the dark. "Be that as it may, I don't think I'm upset about losing *Lorne* so much as I'm upset over the fact that I wasted three years of my life with him. Three years of my life where I could have been looking for or with someone else. Someone I'm *supposed* to be with. My eggs aren't getting any fresher if you know what I mean? I wasted three very viable egg-laying years with him."

"Are you a chicken? Have I been having sex with a chicken all day?"

She snorted. "You know what I mean."

"Birds lay eggs, woman, not people."

"So do crocodiles, frogs, and platypus."

"So are you a reptile, amphibian or marsupial?"

"You know your animals."

"I am a farmer."

Giggling, she took his hand from her breast and brought the pad of his thumb to her mouth, biting it playfully. But he took it a step further, roughly gripped her by the chin, and forced her to turn her head so he could take her mouth possessively with his.

She moaned into his kiss and spun in his arms to straddle him, allowing him to deepen the kiss and push his tongue further into her mouth. His lips caressed hers in a tantalizing, dangerous game and his hard body seemed to mold to every inch of hers.

He tangled his tongue with hers, teasing but demanding at the same time and in a way that was so fantastically infuriating she wanted to scream.

"Asher," she groaned, draping her arms over his muscular shoulders, her fingers toying with the hair at the nape of his neck. He had great hair. Thick, soft and wildly wavy. The hand on her ass squeezed, and the other one moved between their chests to find a nipple and tug.

She gasped against his mouth and smiled. Rocking her hips into his hard cock between them, she lifted up slightly, hovering so the tip notched perfectly at her center, before she slowly sunk down.

"Fuck, woman ..."

"I've never had sex high before," she said before tugging on his lip with her teeth. "Or in a hot tub."

She hadn't been paying much attention, but he'd finished the first joint and snuffed it out in an ashtray, but he had a fresh pre-roll in a package, along with a lighter. He put the new joint between her lips and flicked the lighter until a bright orange flame shone between their faces. He put the flame to the tip of the joint and she sucked in short shallow breaths to get the paper to take the flame.

The tip glowed bright before fading and small coils of smoke drifted up into the night. She sucked in a deeper inhale, pulling the smoke into her lungs and holding it there, keenly aware of Asher's thick cock nestled inside her.

She squeezed around him and he twitched, which made them both smile.

He took the joint from her hands, put it between his lips and inhaled, but he didn't exhale, rather, he took her mouth and pushed the smoke and air into her. It was hot and weird and she got a real heady high from it all. When she drew in a fresh breath, it was like coming up for air after swimming underwater.

But she also wanted more.

They passed the joint back and forth a bit more until it was finished and he snuffed it out in the ashtray. Now, she felt nothing but good. Nothing but incredible. Not even her muscles were sore, and they really should be given how much she'd done yesterday and that she'd sat for hours on that concrete floor in Carolina's stall. But not even her ass hurt—well, not in a bad way.

She'd never been spanked before and certainly hadn't been expecting it, but when Asher's hand met her cheek, it awakened something inside her she had no idea even existed. Immediately, she wanted another and another. The sting, the burn, the spreading heat, and the way it made her pussy absolutely throb was an addiction she had no intention of kicking.

Moving his hand from her ass, he tangled it in her wet hair that hung down her back, and wrapped it around his fist, tugging hard enough to make her tilt her chin and look him in the eye. That snap of pain on her scalp was fabulous and she tightened her muscles around his cock.

A smug grin lazily spread across his face like he knew exactly what she was thinking and how much she liked this rough side to him and sex.

She wanted him to kiss her again. The man definitely knew how to kiss and not just her mouth. The way he'd kissed her pussy that first time in the barn was unlike anything she'd ever experienced. Raw, primal and so greedy. Lorne had never been that way toward her. He'd never feasted on her like he was starving and she was an all you could eat buffet.

His gaze was hot and heavy as he stared down at her with her head tipped up in a slightly uncomfortable way with how tightly he had her by the hair. Why did this turn her on so much?

A small moan worked its way from her throat, and his grin grew even cockier.

Then, because she was going to either break her neck attacking him, or squeeze off his cock, he seemed to understand where she was at and put her out of her beautiful torture, taking her mouth with the same possessiveness he had that first time he kissed her in the barn. Like she was air and he was breathless. Like he owned her.

His hips lifted up beneath her, encouraging her to start moving. With her arms still on his shoulders, she began to bob up and down in his lap, loving how deep she could take him in this position and that his lower belly scraped exquisitely against her clit. The stretch of him that first time he took her was something she would be having many dreams about. He was big, thick and filled her up perfectly. Like he'd been made for her.

Wrapping more of her hair around his fist, he tugged harder until she was forced to break the kiss and look up toward the stars. The clouds had parted with the frigid wind, leaving a midnight sky awash with billions of sparkling stars. It was going to freeze hard tonight, she could already tell.

But in the hot tub they were safe from frostbite and hypothermia. And even if it wasn't a steaming hundred-and-three-degree temperature, they were getting hot and heavy enough on their own to keep the chills at bay.

He dropped his head and sucked on the hollow of her neck, pulling another moan from her throat. His teeth scraped across her clavicle, then he latched onto a nipple with his teeth and tugged.

"Oh God," she crooned, grinding down on his length only to lift up again and swirl his cock head around her sensitive entrance.

He bit her nipple, she slammed back down taking him to the hilt and she shattered. Her screams echoed off the house as she rode his cock like a possessed woman, wringing out every last drop of pleasure from the man beneath her while her pussy clenched and pulsed with her climax.

He released her nipple and reclaimed her mouth, the hold he had on her hair loosening just enough. She spasmed and squeezed around him as the pleasure rocked through her body from her toes to the top of her head and back. The sensations were different than the last few orgasms she'd had. The starbursts behind her eyes were fuzzier, the sensations not as crisp, but they lasted longer. The throbs and sparks of pleasure pulsed like they had their own heartbeat and although they didn't reach a clear almost pointy pinnacle, the length they lasted and the way they crashed and blended together was unlike anything she'd ever experienced. Was this what it was like to orgasm while high?

If so, she wanted to do that again. And again. And again.

Asher still hadn't come when she finally spiraled back down to earth from her foggy climax cloud. Lifting her head from where she'd tucked it into his neck at some point, she opened her eyes and smiled at him lazily.

His grin was pure male triumph. "How was that?" he asked, knowing the answer already.

"That was unlike any orgasm I've ever had before."

"You're really fucking high, aren't you?"

She nodded and grinned again, then a laugh bubbled up through her chest. "Yep."

"I'm glad you're relaxed."

Shimmying in his lap, his cock still in her pussy rock hard and reawakening all her cannabis-stoned neurons, she tilted her head and nipped his jaw. "We still need to get you off."

"I'm going to come down your throat," he said, cradling her face in his hands and pushing his fingers into her hair.

Her eyes widened. He hadn't asked and he'd said it so casually and matter of fact that she was momentarily stunned. And yet, when she rolled the words back through her head, they just turned her on.

The heat in his gaze said he knew it, too.

How did a man she'd only just met know her so damn well already? Know her possibly better than she knew herself? Because she had no idea these were the kinds of things that turned her on.

She nodded just to let him know that she'd heard him and agreed, but inside she was still grappling with his words.

"We're connected Triss ... *literally*. I know how much me saying that just now turned you on. You're also not very good at stealing your emotions. Your eyes are very expressive."

She swallowed hard. "Y-you want to do it here? Right now?" She licked her lips. They'd spent all afternoon in his bedroom but she'd yet to take him in her mouth and the idea of getting to taste him and feel the velvet coated steel of his cock against her tongue was something that had her getting incredibly hot.

Without saying anything, he picked her up off his lap, causing him to slip out of her and he hoisted himself up onto the ledge of the tub.

"But you'll get cold," she said watching as goosebumps emerged on his arms and chest.

"Then you better be quick." He grabbed her hair and wrapped it back around his fist, guiding her mouth down onto his cock. "Easy. Go slow." His words were a dark, delicious purr that sent a physical shiver through her. But she complied and went slow, easing his length into her mouth, swirling her tongue around the crown, enjoying the audible ways he let her know he liked what she was doing.

He pushed her head down more, encouraging her to take him deeper. She did and he knocked her tonsils. Before she could gag, he pulled her hair, drawing her head up.

Growling, she shook her head, gripped his cock with one hand and his balls with the other, and drove her head forward, causing her scalp to burn with how hard that movement pulled on her hair.

His chuckle made her nipples pebble. "Well, okay then," he said, easing up on his grip. She took him to the back of her throat, letting him bottom out, then she contracted her muscles around him in a faux swallow. "Fuck," he gritted.

She lifted her head, swirling her tongue around his shaft as she went, only to scrape her teeth as she reached the head and wedge her tongue into the slit at the top. Then she went back down, using her teeth again, and enjoying the hiss from the man above her and the tug on her hair.

"Easy," he warned.

She tugged on his balls, which caused him to grunt.

She knew he was close when he started to buck up against her face with no rhythm and his thighs began to quiver. She bottomed out twice more, brought him all the way out, sucked hard on his crown, then drove him as far down her throat as she could and he came in a harsh, hair-pulling, profanity ridden canticle that made her smile or at least try to if her mouth hadn't been so full of dick.

She had no choice but to swallow since he was that far down her throat, but she didn't have a problem with it, either.

His cock pulsed in her mouth with every spurt and his balls tightened in her palm. She gave them a gentle tug, and wrapped two fingers below his sac to press up on his perineum, which prompted another rumbly growl to roll through him.

When he was done, he tugged on her hair again to lift her head and he crushed his mouth to hers in an all-consuming, soul-shattering kiss, prying her lips open and tangling his tongue with hers.

His free hand ran down her body, cupping her breasts and rolling her nipple between his fingers before continuing on. Over her belly then circling her waist, the feeling of his rough palm on her skin had her quivering with excitement and ready to ride him all over again.

When he broke the kiss, she was light-headed and more turned on than ever. His eyelids dropped to half-mast and he took her hand. "Let's go to bed, I need to taste you again."

Then he released her hair and helped her climb out of the hot tub. After that, he wrapped her up in a towel and carried her into the house and up to his bed where he did just as he said he would until she passed out with her head on his chest, sated and incredibly happy.

Chapter Twelve

Despite the naked beauty in his bed who he'd much rather have come across his tongue for breakfast, Asher had responsibilities he needed to tend to. Animals to feed and a new foal to check on. So with reluctance in every move he made, he pried his body out of bed and got dressed.

He knew she'd want to help, but she'd done so much over the last two days that Triss deserved to sleep. Besides, she just looked so gorgeous and peaceful with the bedsheet barely covering her body. His cock was getting hard, he needed to get out of there before he climbed back into bed and ducked beneath the covers.

The horses would be getting impatient. He was already half an hour late getting out to feed them.

Tugging on his jeans, he spied his phone flashing on the nightstand and disconnected it from the charger.

It was a message from Nate. *You do know that I have the video feed for the barn on my phone, too, right?*

What the fuck did that mean?

Oh fuck.

Pervert. Asher texted back, heading down the stairs.

Nate texted back right away. A laughing emoji preceded the message *I didn't watch ... for long. But you'd be best to remember that you're not the only one who can see what happens in that barn. That's Hannah's friend.*

Asher shoved his feet into his boots, tugged on his knit cap and pushed his arms into his coat. He didn't bother with gloves and texted his brother as he stalked across the yard toward the barn. It was still dark out, but he could hear the animals starting to wake up. *Yes. Triss. Don't tell Hannah, she'll never shut up about it.*

Too late, bro. Sorry. Got to Oklahoma late last night and checked the barn camera as I sat next to Hannah's hospital bed. She saw it and is SO FUCKING happy.

Asher cringed and heaved open the side door to the barn. Great, just what he needed, his meddling niece doing a little matchmaker dance. She shouldn't be dancing at all since she broke her goddamn ankle and cracked her hip.

Even though he hated talking on the phone more than he hated talking in general, he didn't have the time or hands to be texting back and forth with his brother, so he dialed Nate and put the phone on speaker, tucking it into the breast pocket of his flannel shirt as he went about feeding the horses.

"Good morning, Lothario," Nate teased as he answered the phone. "Those were some skills, bro. Kudos."

Asher rolled his eyes. "You said you didn't watch."

"I said I didn't watch for *long*."

"Carolina foaled yesterday. Filly named Tilly." He didn't want to stick around on the topic of him and Triss in the barn if he could help it. It didn't bother him that much that his brother saw him having sex, but it bothered him that his brother had seen Triss having sex. That was an invasion of *her* privacy, so he'd have to tell her, he just had to figure out how so she didn't get too upset, even though she had every right to.

"Everything good?" Nate asked.

Asher stepped up to the stall with Tilly and her mother. The two were laying down all cuddled up. Tilly's eyes were closed but she was breathing and looked healthy and content. "Carolina did great and Tilly is healthy, just like her mama."

As if she already knew her name, Tilly's eyes opened and she awkwardly stood up and walked her wobbly newborn legs over to the front of the stall where he was. He opened the door and crouched down to give her more attention. "How you doing, baby girl?"

He checked her over, knowing his brother was still on the phone, but also knowing that Nate wouldn't interrupt Asher as he checked out his foal and mare.

He made sure Carolina was doing alright, then mucked their stall first, laid down fresh straw, filled the hay trough and gave them fresh water.

"Doctor wants to keep Hannah in for another couple of days, so I'm going to stick around until she's discharged then drive her back to the ranch. Her spirits are high, but she'll have a bit of a rough road to recover. Girl's bones are made of porcelain."

Asher grunted and went about feeding the rest of the horses, making sure to give the attention-starved Macklin a bit of extra love. "Mercy give you trouble?"

"The Mustang? No, why? He giving you trouble? I mean I know he's a bit of a mean bugger and we haven't been able to collect from him, but no more trouble than the average asshole with a giant dong and balls bigger than his brain."

Asher grunted again. "Yeah, been giving me a bit of a hard time getting him in and out of his stall, but he was great for Triss. Just wondering if it's me or something. What about the other guys?"

Nate made a dismissive noise. "Not that I'm aware of."

"Hmm."

"You gonna be okay by yourself for a couple more days? I didn't plan to be gone this long. I know it's a lot of work for just one person. I told you we shouldn't have given all the hands that time off."

"Triss is helping."

"She is?" His brother sounded genuinely surprised. "Does she have ranch experience?"

"Two weeks at ranch camp when she was a kid, so you know, basically on par with you."

Nate snorted. "You're hilarious. Well, I'm glad that you're not doing it alone, and that you've managed to score a *hump buddy* out of it, too."

"Not you, too," Asher groaned. "Did Hannah use that term and you jumped on it?"

"It's just too perfect."

"You're a child."

Nate was still laughing. "I know. And hey, today is Wednesday."

"So?"

"Hump Day, bro." Nate's chuckle echoed through the barn.

"I'm hanging up now."

"Wait, send me a picture of Tilly, then go hump your new hump buddy, maybe she'll suck that miserable right out of you."

Asher hung up on his brother, but he did go take a picture of Tilly and send it to Nate, along with a picture of Asher giving the camera the finger.

Now he knew exactly how Triss probably felt the other night when her sisters were non-stop ribbing her about saving a horse and riding a cowboy. He'd really had to keep himself from snickering when she corrected them that he was a rancher and *not* a cowboy.

The door from outside opened, bringing with it a cool gust of air and a beautiful, yawning vixen with tired eyes and bite marks on her neck.

His cock jerked in his jeans seeing those bites. His bites. His marks. Because he'd marked her as his. Claimed her.

Even if it was just temporarily.

"Morning, cowboy," she said on another yawn. "You should have woken me up, I would have come help."

"Rancher," he corrected, smiling as he tucked a loose strand of hair behind her ear, his feet had taken him to her before he even knew he was moving. "You just looked so peaceful sleeping. I didn't want to disturb you."

Her brows lifted. "So uh ... last night ..."

"Last night ..." Was she regretting it?

"Was fun."

Oh, thank God. His shoulders left his ears and the tightness that had entered his chest a moment ago disappeared. "It was," he said with a smile. "All of yesterday and last night was a lot of fun."

She dipped her head and glanced up at him from beneath her lashes, her cheeks a cute pink and her smile small. "Umm ... is it wrong of me to assume or ... hope that we can keep doing that while I'm here? That it wasn't just a one-time—well, technically eight-time thing."

Growling, low and deep in his throat, his fingers found their way into her hair and he had her back pressed up against the side of Dare's stall, her eyes wide and full of excitement with just a dash of fear. "Triss," he said, flicking his tongue out and swiping it over her bottom lip, making her shudder against him. "You're in my bed until you leave. Got it?"

Her shiny lips split into a big grin and she nodded. "Got it."

He released her hair and stepped away. "Good. Now go give Tilly some love, she's been asking about you. I'm going to finish up here, then spread you out on the kitchen table and have breakfast."

Her mouth dropped open and her cheeks flushed a sexy rosy color while her eyes burned bright with arousal. "Ummm ... okay then."

Then for good measure, he slapped her ass, told her to "git" which made her squeal, and he finished up what he was doing in the barn with a big fucking smile on his face.

That night, after he plowed the driveway with the plow blade on the front of his truck and they had another pot and whiskey hot tub session, Asher found himself face down on his bed naked, and with a stunning naked woman straddling him and massaging his back with coconut oil. How in the fuck did he get this lucky?

"I know I said I wouldn't pry last night, and I don't intend to but ..." Her soft, hot pussy was burning a hole through his lower back as she worked her thumbs into a tight knot just below his shoulder blades. She'd come to him with coconut oil, having found it in the kitchen. Obviously, it was something Nate bought, since Asher didn't cook with that shit.

He groaned as she leaned forward and shoved her elbow into the knot and put some weight on it.

"But ..." he probed since she'd trailed off.

"But what is the significance of the angel wing tattoo. I mean, if it takes up this much of your body, it has to have a pretty significant meaning, no?"

He was quiet for a while, letting her work her magic on his knots and kinks, since he'd helped her uncover a few of her own kinks earlier that night. His closet lioness liked to be blindfolded and have a little sensory deprivation when he was feeding her his cock, and even more so when he was feasting on her. As much as he loved watching those expressive eyes when she sucked his cock or came undone, it was equally hot having her put that trust in him and allow herself to be blindfolded.

"I'm sorry if I pried," she said quickly after he'd been quiet for way too long. "We don't really know each other and it's not my place. You've seen my tattoo, and I'm sure you can guess that it's for me and my sisters. We each have one."

"A friend died," he finally said, fighting to get each word past the lump in his throat. "A few friends actually. It just honors them."

His entire back would be covered in wings if he wanted to honor and re-member each and every man he knew who had given his life for his country—or taken his own life when his country didn't give a shit about him after he got home. Because that had certainly been the case with Brandon. The shit he saw had haunted him so badly he took his own life, leaving his wife and daughter all alone.

But he didn't want to pick at those scars right now, and she was right, they really didn't know each other and it wasn't her place. So he didn't say anything else and she didn't pry.

He liked that about her. She was smart and didn't push. Even though she was a bit of a chatterbox at times, she also seemed to know when a conversation was over—something his niece Hannah hadn't managed to learn in her thirty-two years.

"So what are you going to do when you get home?" he asked, his voice scratchy with fatigue, even though his cock was getting hard beneath him from the way she was rubbing her cleft against his back. Every so often when she leaned over, her tits would brush his back, too, and she'd suck in a breath which only made him get harder.

Her sigh was weary and she paused her thumb on a knot in his mid-back. "I don't know. Hannah had a friend move all my stuff to a storage locker. And I'm having an almost impossible time trying to find a place in my price range or in a decent neighborhood. I might have to live in an Airbnb for a few months. They can come pretty reasonable, and since it's the off-season, I might be able to find something decent." She started working on that knot again. "I'll tell you one thing, though, I'm going to be using my Instant Pot every damn day."

"I don't know what that is."

"Like a Crock Pot but it does a million more things and is a million times better."

He grunted.

"I'm also going to map out a new route to work that doesn't involve me driving past my old apartment since it's pretty central and on a main road, so you almost have to drive past it to get to my office. But I'll detour five minutes out of my way through suburbia if I have to. I'll brave those speed bumps and wave to the soccer moms."

He snorted. "Isn't that letting them win?"

"Who, the soccer moms?"

"No. Douchebag and Moonbeam."

It was her turn to snort. "Echo. But I like Moonbeam better. And no. It's called self-preservation. I don't need to unnecessarily torture myself by driving past Lorne and Moonbeam's house when I don't have to. If I saw them, it would just make me mad, and I don't like being mad. I don't want frown lines."

"All I have are frown lines."

"I'm aware."

In a quick and agile move that had her squeaking in surprise, he flipped her off him and onto her back and had settled himself on top of her and between her thighs. "Are you calling me a grumpy fuck?"

She grinned up at him. "Sexy and grumpy, but yes, you're a grumpy fuck." Then she did something that made his brain short-circuit and not necessarily in the sexy, orgasmic kind of way. She rubbed her nose against his. "But I happen to like the sexy-grumpy combo, and your frown lines just make you look distinguished and dangerous." Her smile made his heart start to hammer wildly in his chest, and when she giggled all sweet and girly, he thought he was going to black out.

Oh fuck, he was having a panic attack.

Rolling off her to his back, he placed the heels of his palms against his eyes.

"Hey," Triss pressed a cool, delicate hand to his chest, "are you okay?"

Clenching his jaw until he thought he might chip a tooth, he sucked in air through his nose hard and breathed out with just as much force.

"Asher ... you're scaring me. Are you okay?"

What could he say to her?

No, you just showed me affection and your softness and kindness scared the shit out of me. That I'm worried I'm going to react in a way that frightens you when we least expect it.

Because that was what it was. She was so sweet, soft, and kind, but with a spine of steel and when she rubbed her nose against his, an innocuous gesture if ever there was one, it made his heart thunder in his chest and his gut began to spin. The last thing he ever wanted to do was scare or hurt this beautiful woman, and that's exactly what he knew he'd do if he let her get too close.

She'd shown up on his doorstep for a reason, but was it to disrupt his predictable, safe world? A world where he kept people at arm's length for a reason. Because he wasn't sure if he could do that if it was. He liked his women like Teflon, easy to peel off. If they got sticky, they would start to see the real him, the broken him and that was the last thing anyone deserved to see.

"Hey," she pressed her warm body up against his, "tell me what you need. Want me out of your bed? Do you need space, just say the word. I won't be offended or hurt."

He shook his head. Normally, his instinct would have been to go somewhere where he was alone and in the quiet, but having her near, with her heat and softness pressed against him was actually calming him faster than a silent, empty pasture ever had.

Slowly, his heart began to settle and his breathing slowed down. He wasn't ready to open his eyes, though, and face her, so he kept his hands over his face for a full minute longer before slowly peeling them away and glancing at her.

And holy fuck, the look that greeted him wasn't at all what he was expecting.

He was sure he'd see fear, worry, and probably even confusion. But her eyes gave him none of that.

Rather, she met him with a twisted lipped smile and relief in those soulful brown orbs. "Hey," she said quietly. "Welcome back."

"Hey," he murmured. "Sor—"

"So ... I'm kind of hungry. I'm going to run downstairs and do up a plate of something to nibble on. That sound good to you?"

He blinked several times. Why wasn't she asking what happened? Why wasn't she slinking away from him in fear?

Slowly, he nodded. "Yeah."

She slid out of bed and tugged his white T-shirt over her body. It hit her knees and she looked fucking stunning in it with her hair a wild mess of waves over her shoulders.

"Find us something funny to watch on the television. Maybe A Christmas Story, since it *is* Christmas Eve after all." Then with a smile that made his chest get warm, she padded downstairs.

He stared at the doorway she'd just walked through for nearly a minute, still not able to entirely believe what just happened.

He'd had a panic attack. He'd had them before, so he knew what they felt like. But he'd never come down from one that fast or had anybody react to him in that way. She wasn't scared, was barely even phased, and she didn't push him to talk about it.

It was like she knew precisely what he needed more than he did.

He'd never met a woman like that before. He'd never met a person who was able to unflappably help him through a panic attack. Even a small one like that.

Was this why she'd shown up on his doorstep?

Was Triss the breath of fresh air he didn't even know he needed? And if she was, how in the hell was he going to let her walk out of his life when she finally needed to head home?

Chapter Thirteen

Asher had a panic attack.

That much was clear, but what she couldn't figure out was why.

She knew from working with clients that the best thing to do when someone had a panic attack was to just let them know they weren't alone—unless that was what they preferred, though most people didn't—and let your touch help calm down their parasympathetic nervous system. If she thought it might work, she would have climbed on top of Asher and hugged him, but she didn't think he would understand what she was trying to do and probably freak out even more.

As a speech pathologist, she wasn't just confined to working with people who had stutters and lisps. She also worked with people of all ages who had difficulty eating and swallowing, whether from trauma, brain injuries, dementia, neurological impairments and other compromising issues. In addition to that, she was trained in cognitive-communication disorders including social communication skills, reasoning, problem solving and executive functions.

Over the last few years, she'd had an influx of brain injury clients, several of whom were veterans, and although most were fairly mild-mannered, a few had aggression issues and were prone to violent outbursts, particularly if they got frustrated or were triggered. This led her to take extra training courses and workshops over the years on how to handle panic attacks, aggression, and violence. Non-violent crises intervention was something she routinely had to take every couple of years in order to maintain her license.

And not that she thought Asher would get violent, but she had to be prepared for it. She had no idea what his triggers were.

Obviously, she'd said something or done something to send him into a panic, but he wasn't in the right headspace to talk about it.

She made her way into the kitchen and flicked on a light. The wood stove was keeping everything warm, so the only time goosebumps prickled along her legs was when she opened the fridge.

Quietly, alone with her thoughts, she prepared a small plate of cheese, sliced apples and grapes. This was unlike any Christmas Eve she'd ever had, but it certainly wasn't the worst. Far from it in fact.

Asher and the ranch were the perfect distraction from her chaotic, confused life back in Connecticut.

She was falling more and more in the love with the ranch with each moment, particularly Macklin, Tilly and Carolina. But even Fumble, that rogue goat, was starting to warm up to her and had head-butted her a few times for some head scratched between his horns.

Against Asher's reluctance, she was the one to lead Mercy out into the corral so that they could muck his stall. And the black Mustang with the shiny mane and intelligent eyes gave her zero problems. He even stuck around her, nuzzling her head with his nose when she stayed in the corral.

Asher called him a jerk. She just called Mercy misunderstood.

Yes, this ranch, the dozens of hearts beating on it, and the piling snow were exactly what she needed. It was the lacquer and gold dust for her Kintsugi heart. She wouldn't be defined by the damage Lorne had done to her, but rather, she would use it to make herself stronger and more resilient.

After tidying up in the kitchen, with the plate in hand, she was about to shut off the light when a broad, shadowy figure stepped forward from the living room.

"I'm sorry," he said, wearing nothing but his black boxer briefs and looking mighty delicious, if not a little rattled and disheveled.

She shook her head. "Nothing to apologize for."

He held her gaze for a long moment, his eye searching hers, confusion and awe mixing in the dark blue.

"Nate saw us," he finally said.

Her brows scrunched. "Huh?"

"In the barn. He has the camera footage sent to his phone, too, and he and Hannah saw us ... you know ... yesterday."

It took her a second to understand what he was saying, but when it finally clicked, her eyes went wide and she nearly dropped the plate of food. Setting it down on the counter, she started to slowly nod. "I see."

"I don't care that he saw me, but it was an invasion of your privacy and you have a right to know."

Was this what had triggered his panic attack?

No, that didn't add up.

Her head continued to bob. "So ... what did they see?"

He shrugged. "I don't know. Nate wouldn't look for long. He'd see what we were doing then turn off the feed. He's not a pervert like that." He scratched the back of his neck. "At least I don't think. And I'm Hannah's uncle for fuck's sake, so he wouldn't let her watch."

"Okay ..."

His chest lifted and fell on a dramatic sigh. "I just needed you to know. That's not something that should be kept from you."

Twisting her lips, she mulled over this revelation in her head for a moment.

Did she really care that Asher's brother—a guy she'd never met before—and her best friend saw her having sex for probably all of thirty seconds? Sure, there was a modicum of embarrassment trickling through her, but for the most part, the idea of it just made her hot.

She wasn't interested in making a sex tape and posting it on the internet for every Jack to jack-off to, but the idea that they'd been "caught" had its appeal.

Eventually, she lifted her shoulder in a shrug. "Well, at least we gave them a show, huh?"

His eyes went wide. "You're not mad?"

"No. It's actually kind of hot if you think about it. I mean, I doubt your brother is gonna leak it to the press, and even if he did, we're nobodies."

"He's not going to leak it."

"So we have nothing to worry about."

Heat flared in his eyes and he slowly stalked toward her, the tent in his boxers was growing and she had a hard time peeling her gaze away from it. "You're really fucking cool, you know that?" he said, reaching her and circling her waist with his hands.

"I have been told such things from time to time, yes." She tipped her head up and pinned her gaze on his. "Thank you for telling me, though. Not all guys would have been so open or understanding about my privacy and right to know."

Lifting her up, he plunked her bare ass on the countertop and his hands slid beneath the hem of his shirt that she was wearing, tracing up her thighs and sending hot sparks of desire zapping through her.

"I'm not a big talker," he said, his voice deep, gravelly and so damn sexy it made her nipples pebble.

"I've noticed."

"I like the quiet."

"The quiet can be good."

"I prefer to *show* how I'm feeling, rather than say it out loud."

Sliding her tongue along her bottom lip, she let her gaze drift down to his erection and brushed it with her hand through the soft fabric. "I can see how you're feeling pretty clearly right now."

He shook his head. "No. I mean *really* show you." Then he dropped to a crouch, pulled her ass to the edge of the counter, and went ears-deep between her legs.

Her head fell back and knocked the cupboard as her fingers wove their way into his hair and she held him in place.

Yeah, the man wasn't much of a talker, but he was sure talented with that mouth of his. And to be honest, talking was overrated when they could do things like this.

He pushed two fingers into her channel and pumped, coaxing that simmering orgasm that burbled and bubbled right at the surface.

She squirmed against him, loving it when he sucked on her clit hard enough she thought he was trying to remove it from her body. Then he'd ease up and waggle his tongue over it, sweeping that strong, limber muscle up between her folds. He chased his tongue with his stubbled chin and she nearly lose her damn head.

He knew the precise spot to hit her clit and where to press inside her that had her bucking against his face, her leg jerking and stars bursting behind her closed eyes.

But he also knew just how hard to press and suck to *not* tip her over the mountain top. To keep her riding the edge, it was decadent torture that infuriated her just as much as it turned her on.

It all felt so incredible, and yet she knew what waited for her with just a little shove.

Pure bliss.

"Asher," she crooned, tightening her grip on his hair and pressing her pussy harder against his face.

He ignored her and kept eating.

"Asher ... dear God."

He didn't let up, if anything, he ate with more determination, more vigor, and when his other finger pressed at her ass, then gathered some of her juices only to press again, she was biting her lip too damn hard to say anything.

That was until he breached her tight hole and the unfamiliar pressure and pleasure sent her headfirst into the most epic, brain-exploding orgasm of her entire life.

His suction on her clit had her lifting off the counter, pressing her back against the cupboard to arch into his face, while his fingers inside her pressed up hard on her G-spot until she felt like she needed to pee.

But it was that finger in her ass—something she'd never done before—that had sent her hurdling over the edge of the cliff and straight into the clouds filled with rainbows, singing angels, and cotton candy craping unicorns.

Her limbs went stiff and she yanked harder on his hair, pressing him against her pussy until he probably couldn't breathe, but she didn't care. And he didn't seem to, either.

Only when the orgasm that felt like it would never end finally ended, did she slump back to the counter and begin her gentle float back to earth, waving goodbye to the unicorns and angels.

She released his hair with a murmured apology that was strictly said to be polite, she didn't mean it—he yanked her hair all the time and never apologized—but she kept her eyes closed, watching the last of the fireworks fade on the back of her eyelids.

He withdrew his fingers from her pussy then her ass and a second later she heard the faucet running.

But she didn't move.

She couldn't.

She was jelly-boned and really, really happy about it.

Moments later, big, strong arms scooped her up. "Grab the plate," he murmured, his voice raspy and causing her pussy to clench.

She opened her eyes sleepily, grabbed the plate of snacks and allowed the sexy rancher with the pain behind his eyes to carry her upstairs to his bed.

He'd managed to find A Christmas Story, but she only made it twenty minutes before she was passed out in his arms, her head on his chest and the steady beat of his heart beneath her ear.

Tomorrow was Christmas and although there was no tree downstairs, she hadn't unpacked her stocking from her suitcase and the man with his arm around her wouldn't be dressing up in red velour and donning a white beard, she couldn't think of anywhere she'd rather be. This was exactly what she needed. She just hoped that when the time came to go home, she could take her Kintsugi heart—with all its cracks and battered history—with her and not leave it here with a man who had no idea what to do with it.

She woke up with Asher's face back between her legs. The best way in the world to wake up, hands down. And after she came, he poked his head out from the covers and flashed her a rare, bright smile. "Merry Christmas, gorgeous."

She grinned back at him, her body pliant and muscles deliciously achy. "Good morning to you, cowboy."

"Rancher," he corrected. "Afraid I don't have a gift for my sexy squatting house guest but feel free to use me and abuse me all day. I'm yours to ride any way you please."

The demons that had possessed him last night seemed to have disappeared on the icy wind. That or they were buried under a foot of snow and would re-emerge when the world started to thaw. But either way, the man who smiled at her with his lips and chin glistening from her release was far less haunted than the man she'd fallen asleep next to last night.

She was falling for both men, but she liked this side of him. It seemed to involve less of his energy to be happy.

"Well, I might just take you up on that amazing Christmas present," she said, climbing over him to straddle his body, but then shimmying her way down so she was face to face with his cock. "But I think you should open my gift first before I open any more of yours. It's only fair."

His thumb gently brushed her chin and encouraged her to open her mouth. "Open up, pretty girl," he ordered, his demanding tone sending a flutter of desire through her. She did as he said and took him to the back of her throat. His fingers threaded their way into her hair and he set a pace with her head that he liked. "Yeah, that's it," he murmured. "Merry fucking Christmas."

After Asher's orgasm and then one more for her where she sat on his face and rode his short beard and lips like a bucking bronco, they both reluctantly slid out of bed and went to go feed the animals. Since Asher didn't bother to put up a tree, Santa would have skipped this house, therefore *not* leaving treats for the animals. This was something she felt the need to remind him of, which just made him snort and smirk.

"I'll give you a big ol' piece of wood in the living room, woman," he'd said before tackling her against Hula-Hoop's stall and kissing her breathless and silly. "Don't need a tree covered in lights."

Macklin had made a noise of protest when he saw Triss giving her affections to Asher and not him, so she pushed her sexy rancher away and went to go give some love to Macklin. "And a Merry Christmas to you, handsome," she said, kissing Macklin's nose before holding out her palm with some carrot pieces and apple slices on it. He ate them from her happily, his big, velvety lips gentle on her hand. He nudged her with his nose and she kissed him again. "I can't move into your stall, I'm sorry. Unlike you, I don't like sleeping standing up."

The horse almost seemed to growl like he didn't think that was an excuse.

"He's an attention whore with everyone, but I've never seen him get this possessive of a person before," Asher said, wandering up to where Triss was scratching Macklin between the ears. "I think you've made an impression on all the animals. Even Fumble has stopped trying to escape, and that goat's always looking for greener pastures."

She beamed at him.

"Wanna help me get Mercy into the corral so we can muck his stall?"

Her eyes widened. Yesterday she'd had to browbeat Asher into letting her lead Mercy. Even then, his disposition had been the definition of cantankerous when she proved him wrong and Mercy was a sweet gentleman with her.

It seemed like Asher was finally coming around and believing in her being the Mercy whisperer.

"Sure," she said, deciding not to rub his nose in anything since they had a good vibe going this morning, and it didn't seem like his demons from last night had come back wearing elf ears.

They went to Mercy's stall and the big misunderstood lug hung his head over the door. "Merry Christmas, big guy," she said, kissing his nose and giving him a scratch between his ears. He ate up the attention, and of course, Macklin down the way made a huff of protest. Mercy glanced up at Macklin and she could have sworn the two had a silent showdown with Macklin making another huff and disappearing into his stall. "Boys, boys, don't be like that. There is plenty of me to go around."

She'd set the metal bucket of carrots and apple on a shelf and when she turned to grab it, she accidentally knocked it over instead, sending it to the ground in a horrible, noisy clatter.

"What the fuck?" Asher roared from where he was grabbing the halter beside Mercy's stall, his hands pressed to his ears. "Be more fucking careful! FUCK! FUCKING HELL!"

Mercy had startled at the bucket dropping, thrashing his head side to side, and neighing loudly, but when Asher hollered the horse actually start to kick and stomp in his stall. His head continued to thrash and his sounds of distress were increasing.

Not sure what to do, she bent down to grab the bucket and the strewn carrots and apples. She lifted her head to apologize to Asher but he was gone, the only way she knew where he'd gone was by the sudden sub-zero gust of wind that entered the barn.

"Shhh," she said softly, turning her attention back to Mercy, and holding up an apple slice. "Shhh, big guy, it's okay."

Mercy was breathing deeply, snort spraying out of his nose. His eyes were wild, but he was focusing them on her more and more. She lifted her hand and touched his neck, the only part of him she could without actually getting into the stall with him.

But that seemed to be enough and he turned to face her, snorting and snuffling and breathing heavy.

"It's okay," she cooed. "It's okay. That was a loud noise, followed by another loud noise, but it's okay. Shhhhh." She petted his neck and when he gave her more access, she stroked his face and pressed her forehead to the side of his face. "Shhhh, big guy. Shhhhh."

She stood there with her eyes closed, forehead to Mercy's cheek until he'd stopped panting and moving about. She held her palm out in front of his nose with the apple slices on it and his lips gently gripped the apple and pulled them into his mouth.

"That's it. Good boy. Good. Just a few big noises, but nothing to worry about. It's okay." Running her hand down his neck back and forth, she continued to murmur similar things to Mercy until he'd completely calmed down. She gave him more apple and attention until he seemed to have almost forgotten entirely what happened and was sniffing around her waist and neck in search of more treats when she cut him off. "I need to save some for the other horses," she said on a laugh as he sniffed her hair and gently head-butted her. "I can't be accused of playing favorites. You may have put Macklin in his place just now, but the guy has a serious crush on me, you better watch out."

At that Mercy just snorted like he'd like to see Macklin try, and shook his head.

Asher still hadn't returned, but she didn't let that stop her and she went about giving Christmas treats to the rest of the horses. Then she visited the donkey, the pony, and the miniature horses, returning to the main part of the barn with an empty bucket, straw in her hair, and goat hoof prints on her thighs.

Asher was also back.

He was mucking out Greenleigh's stall while Greenleigh munched on hay and paid him no mind.

Slowly, cautiously, she approached the stall with the open door, standing out of the way of the horse shit that was being tossed through into the wheelbarrow.

She cleared her throat. "Umm ..."

She knew he knew she was there. His back stiffened and his shoulders tensed. But he didn't say anything, didn't acknowledge her.

"I uh ... I think we could probably take Mercy to the corral now, he's calmed down."

But have you calmed down?

His reaction to the loud noise had to be PTSD-related. She wasn't an idiot and had worked with veterans with PTSD before. A client she started working with last year developed, lung, throat, and mouth cancer from inhaling smoke from the burn pits in Iraq and he had to basically re-learn how to talk, eat and swallow after his surgery. He had severe PTSD and they had to conduct their sessions in a room with minimal light, and she had to keep her voice low when she spoke. Noah was doing very well now, but he still had issues with loud noises—even his boisterous children bothered him—and he preferred to go out at night rather than during the day.

Something traumatic must have happened to Asher for him to react that way. It also made her wonder if he'd reacted this way around Mercy before and Mercy associated Asher with the outburst and that was why he was so anxious around him.

He finished cleaning out Greenleigh's stall and stepped back out into the barn, finally tipping his blue gaze up to her. "Fine."

Fine?

Fine!

She was giving this man a lot of leeway, but she deserved more than just

"Fine."

Grinding her teeth, she took a few deep fortifying breaths. At the very least he owed her an apology for the way he spoke to her. It was understandable how something like a metal bucket falling over would trigger him, but he said some pretty mean stuff to her, too, and he needed to own it.

Plopping her hands on her hips she stared at him. "That's it?"

He grunted and walked past her toward Mercy's stall.

"That's it?" she said again, this time louder and turning around to face him, even though he was still showing her his back. "I get you were triggered by the loud noise, and I'm not going to pry about why, but you owe me an apology."

He spun around to face her, anger in his eyes. "Fine. I'm sorry. Happy?" He turned back around, heading toward Mercy's stall.

She ran after him, got ahead, and stopped in front of him so he was forced to stop, too. "No, I'm not actually. I get that you *think* you're broken, and you've probably experienced some trauma and have PTSD, but that doesn't give you the right to be an asshole and *not* genuinely apologize for it. It doesn't give you license to be a jerk and think you can get away with it. What happened with the bucket was a pure accident, what happened after that *wasn't*. And what's happening now, sure as hell isn't, either."

"You don't like it, don't like who I am ...? Then you're free to fucking leave anytime you want." He swept his hand out and pointed toward the road. "I can call you a cab right now."

She nodded and rolled her lips inward. "Is that what we're doing then? You're *scaring* me off so that you don't have to run the risk of someone actually seeing your flaws ... of seeing the real you?" She laughed. "I mean, yeah, you've got the grumpy, war-ravaged soldier schtick down pat, not gonna lie, but you're laying on that anger at the world, not worthy of love or happiness thing a little thick right now, don't you think?"

Fury flickered in his blue eyes and his nostrils flared. "What the fuck gives you the right?"

She shrugged, ready to spar with him if it meant finally getting to see a few cracks in the reinforced stone wall that he'd constructed around himself. "I dunno maybe the fact that I'm a total stranger, have known you for like three days and yet I can pretty much read you like a book? Or the fact that just because I'm a speech pathologist doesn't mean I haven't studied psychology, trauma, and PTSD. I don't just work with kids with lisps, you know. I work with all kinds. Veterans, the elderly, adults with brain injuries. I've met people who had seen some scary shit, so I know what it looks like when they're triggered."

His lip curled up into a snarl, but she rolled her eyes and that seemed to actually diffuse some of his ire. Had nobody ever stood up to Asher before?

"I might let you throw me against the wall and spank my ass, but there's a difference between consensual disrespect for pleasure and blatant disrespect where you're intentionally hurting me. I'm not looking for a future from you, but I am looking for some goddamn respect."

"So what, you're just going to leave me here high and dry?" The desperation in his voice almost had her breaking her composure and wrapping her hands around his waist. But she held her ground.

"Well, for starters, you just told me to leave. I haven't said a damn word about leaving. All I've asked for is an apology and some respect. Secondly, no, I don't quit a job before I'm done. But I also don't back down to bullies." Then at that, she turned around, stepped up to Mercy's stall, opened the door, and stepped inside. She'd rather take her chances with the misunderstood man with a silky mane, than the brooding sexy asshole who was glaring daggers at her.

At least that's what she kept telling herself.

Chapter Fourteen

"Hand me his halter," Triss said, holding out her hand from where she stood in Mercy's stall, talking gently to the beast and petting his neck.

Anger flared hot and nauseating inside Asher, but he did as she requested and handed her the halter that was hanging up beside his stall.

She put it on Mercy just like Asher had taught her, and the horse gave her zero problems.

"Excuse me," she said, leading Mercy out of the stall and into the barn. "We'll be in the corral." Then, not bothering to look at Asher again, but telling him with the flick of her hair and the sway of her hips that he could shovel shit for all she cared, she walked past him toward the corral.

Growling at the infuriating woman with the rocking ass, he stalked back to Greenleigh's stall where he had the wheelbarrow and wheeled it down to Mercy's stall.

Where the fuck did she get off talking to him like that?

More importantly, why the hell did it turn him on?

She had no right.

He had PTSD from that explosion—and many others like it—in Iraq and loud noises were a trigger for him.

She should understand that.

She does, and is giving you a huge by, what she's not letting you get away with is how you spoke to her.

Yeah, he'd overreacted and was a dick, but owning up to his reaction, to his trauma, just made him feel like such a failure. He'd failed Mauricio when he left him in that hospital to die. And now he was failing at keeping his shit together. It was a fucking bucket that fell for Christ's sake, not a goddamn grenade.

He didn't want her to go, but it seemed like the safest option at this point.

Safest for you, maybe. She doesn't seem scared at all.

Fuck. Their morning had started out so great, even after his stupid panic attack last night, and now he went and fucked it all up by treating her like crap.

He finished cleaning out Mercy's stall, filled the trough with hay, and replenished his water before he moved on to a few more horses' stalls. He really did need to get them all into the corral for some exercise.

After about thirty minutes of shoveling shit and mental flagellation, he made his way to the corral where the tinkling sound of laughter drew him like the Pied Piper.

"What a pretty boy you are," Triss said as Mercy came happily trotting over to her, gently head-butted her, then began to nuzzle her head with his. "And very loving, too."

Asher cleared his throat which drew both Triss's and Mercy's attention.

Mercy snorted, made a noise of frustration, then left Triss and trotted over to the other side of the corral. But he kept his eye on Asher and Triss.

Oh great, another horse possessive of Triss. First Macklin and now this moody bugger.

Shoving his hands into his pockets, his gaze on his boots, he approached her. "I uh ... I owe you an apology." His head tipped up and he met her eyes with his. Patience and kindness shone back at him in the soft, beautiful brown. "I overreacted when the bucket fell ... as you guessed, loud noises are a trigger for me. But I shouldn't have reacted the way I did and I'm sorry." He swallowed.

"Truly."

Pressing her lips into a flat line, she blinked at him.

He held his breath and watched her shoulders slump and a small smile slowly curl her lips. "Thank you. I'm sure that wasn't easy, so I appreciate it and I believe that your apology is genuine."

Glancing at Mercy who was watching them with a wary eye, she stepped out of the corral and toward Asher, invading his space and bringing her subtle floral scent with her. Her hands found his waist and she tipped her head up to look at him. "I'm here if you want to talk, but I'm not going to push. We don't know each other. This is just a fun Christmas fling, so if you want to keep it light, then we can keep it light."

He nodded. But the weird churning in his gut when she called it *just a fling* was interesting.

Jerking his chin toward Mercy, he asked, "How's he doing?"

She shrugged. "Fine. I calmed him down. He really is a big softy, you know. Maybe just a bit misunderstood ..." She tightened her hold on him which caused him to glance down at her again. "All the most interesting and complex guys are, right?"

He scoffed. "Not sure if I'm interesting or complex. Not even sure if I'm misunderstood, but sure."

"I was referring to the horse, not you," she teased, her giggle making his heart light and the rest of his body buoyant. God, it felt good to not be so bogged down with the anger that seemed to constantly be riding on his shoulders like two asshole obese devils whispering stupid shit in his ears.

"Oh were you?" he asked, with a growl, backing her up until her butt hit the outside of the corral, then dropping his mouth to take hers, gripping her chin and taking control of their kiss.

She moaned into his mouth and he swallowed the sound, his cock jerked in his jeans and he pressed his hips against her.

He didn't even here the sneaky bastard until he was right there behind her, making noises of protest and possessiveness, snorting and nudging the back of Triss's head with his nose.

She broke their kiss and laughed, turning in Asher's arms to face Mercy. "Jealous, handsome?" Mercy grunted. "Trust me, of the two of you, I'll always pick you. No competition."

"Hey," Asher spun her back around to face him. "Just 'cause his dick is bigger doesn't mean you get to toss me into the manure pile. Unless bestiality is another one of your closet kinks."

Her eyes went wide and he grinned. "Uh, *my* closet kinks?"

"Yeah. I know my kinks. No need keep 'em in the closet. You, on the other hand, appear to have no idea you liked being spanked, blindfolded or dominated. Am I right?"

She bit her lip and her eyes went wide and doll-like. "Uh ..."

"Do you think you'd like being tied up, too? I've got some silk ties I haven't worn in years that would look so fucking sexy around your wrists and ankles while you're spread wide on my bed."

Her throat moved hard and she swallowed before licking her lips. "Ummm ..."

God, could his smile get any bigger? It was hurting his damn cheeks.

Thank fuck she forgave so easily.

He definitely wasn't ready to let her go, and even though he knew their time together was temporary, he planned to make the most of it.

Dipping his mouth to her neck, he pressed kisses before scraping his teeth across her rapidly beating pulse point. "I bet you have a lot of closet kinks we could explore."

"You think so?"

"Only one way to find out."

"We're not done out here." Her head lolled to the side, granting him better access to her slender neck. "We have animals to care for."

With a grumble, he nipped her jaw. "Must you always be so practical?"

WHITLEY COX

Laughing, she tore herself away from him and stepped back into the corral. Mercy was still right there, giving Asher the stink-eye. "The faster we finish chorin', the faster you can give me another Christmas present."

"Did you just say *chorin*'?"

She beamed at him. "That's what we're doing, right? Chorin'?"

Snorting, he nodded. "Yeah, it just sounds funny coming from a little city slicker like you."

She tipped an imaginary Stetson at him. "You're quickly turning this city slicker into a country girl with all these beautiful animals and orgasms there, cowboy."

"Rancher."

She petted Mercy and led him easily out of the corral, throwing Asher a wink as she headed back into the barn. "Potato, poh-tah-to, right, Mercy?"

Now why did he not hate the idea of her becoming a country girl, and more importantly, why did he really want to be the one to help her achieve it and do it right here on his ranch?

After making sure the animals were all fed, brushed and given the attention they needed, Asher apologized by way of three screaming orgasms to Triss in the shower, on the bathroom counter and in his bed.

She would say he was redeemed and then some, especially since she had to hang onto the wall when she went downstairs since her legs were made of Jell-O.

"I just got a text from my sister, Oona, so I'm going to video chat with her in my room," Triss said to Asher, who was busy in the kitchen. He said that, although he didn't have a turkey or any of the trimmings, he did have two nice steaks, potatoes, and some broccoli that he could cook for Christmas dinner.

Triss's mouth watered at the thought of a baked potato loaded with sour

118

cream and bacon bits, so she nodded eagerly at his suggestion.

He also boasted a "kickass" rub which was going to "knock her socks off" so he was busy in the kitchen doing that.

"Sounds good," he said over his shoulder.

It was weird stepping into her bedroom, well, the guest room that was *her* room for the duration of her stay. It no longer felt like *her* space.

How could that be when she'd only been here three nights and barely knew Asher?

Ignoring the buzzing and tingly along her arms at that weird feeling of belonging more in Asher's bed than in the guest room, she opened up her tablet and called her sister.

Oona answered on the third ring. "Merry Christmas, you sexy beast," Oona said with a grin. Her eyes were slightly glazed over and she had a red and silver tinsel tiara on her head.

"Oon, have you been drinking?"

"Sure fucking have, big sis. Rum and eggnog and some delicious mulled wine. One of my colleagues is having a 'friends Christmas dinner' for all of us losers without families to go visit."

"At least you're not alone," Triss said, grabbing the blanket draped over the bottom of the bed and snuggling her legs under it. "I miss you."

"Miss you, too," Oona said, sipping from a wine glass. Triss could see a wedge of orange and a cinnamon stick floating in the dark red liquid. "Have you had a good day so far?"

"So far so good," Oona said, then she pouted. "Rayma and Pasha told me Lorne dumped you. That motherfucker. I've already left a one-star Yelp review on his and that Echo bitch's restaurant. I've gotten my friends here to do the same."

Triss tried to hide the smile that threatened to curl her mouth. "You guys really shouldn't do that. We don't want to hurt the owners of the restaurant or the rest of the staff. It's not their fault Lorne is a dick."

"We thought of that," Oona said, her smile sly and proud. "We specifically said the food by *Lorne Waring* was gross. That when he was in the kitchen, we'd rather eat a French fry we found under the passenger seat of our car."

"Oon ..." Triss chuckled. "He's going to know I had something to do with it."

She shrugged. "Then he shouldn't have dumped you in such a dickish fashion. We protect what's ours. Mieka left a review, too."

"How is Mieks?"

"Living it up on a cruise ship and banging first officers. How do you think she is?"

Triss rolled her eyes. "Right. I forget that our sister, the dancer, is gorgeous, bendy and the life of the party."

"Who can drink every single one of us under the table and not gain a fucking pound."

"Don't remind me," Triss said blandly.

"But, back to you being dumped by the douche. How are you doing?" Oona's brown eyes took a second to focus, but eventually they did and concern shone back at Triss. "Rayma said you're in Colorado with a naked cowboy?"

Triss rolled her eyes again. "Yes, I'm in Colorado, on a ranch and he's a *rancher* not a cowboy and last I checked he was wearing clothes."

"But not all the time, right?" Oona's thick brows bobbed.

Triss's face grew warm and she could see in her tiny picture on the bottom of the screen that her cheeks were getting pink.

"Ooooh, girl, get some Christmas booty, you deserve it," Oona cheered, lifting her glass in a toast before taking a big sip. "I expect at least one picture, though. I mean it. It didn't happen unless there is proof. Preferably a naked picture, but I'll settle for shirtless."

"I'm not taking a picture of him naked and sending it to you."

"I said I'd settle for shirtless, you prude."

"Have you talked to mom and dad?"

Oona nodded, tucking a strand of her dark brown hair behind her ear. "Yeah, they're having a blast with Aunt Georgina in Florida. Dad was wearing a Hawaiian printed shirt and mom was drinking from a Tiki torch-style mug. I've never seen them that relaxed. It was weird."

Triss's brows scrunched. "Yeah, that doesn't sound like them at all."

Oona scrunched up her face. "I know, right?"

"I went to Baltimore for one night before I flew out to Colorado. One night in my old childhood bedroom is one night too many. Next time I go, I'm going to get a hotel room."

Oona nodded. "Let me know the next time you go and I'll fly down, too, and we can split a hotel room. Also, that way I don't have to visit them alone." She shuddered.

Triss could nearly feel her sister's shudder across the miles. Or maybe that was just a shudder of her own. She definitely wouldn't be going back to visit her parents without sibling reinforcement, that was for damn sure. And a hotel where she could drink *after* the visit, since her parents didn't keep alcohol in the house.

"Can you imagine if that Tiki mug has booze in it and Dad is actually getting sloshed?" Oona said with excitement.

Triss scoffed. "I bet it's water, or at the very most ginger ale."

Oona frowned. "You're probably right. God, our parents are such squares."

"Is Mieka somewhere where I can call her," Triss asked, eager to get off the topic of their parents.

Her sister shook her head. "Tomorrow she will be, so try her then. She's off partying in like Martinique or something." Her eyes rolled. "That bitch."

Triss chuckled. "I mean, she's got no ass, so ..."

"Right, that flat-ass bitch. Fuck her and her amazing life. I love her though, but still fuck her."

They both laughed and chatted a bit longer, but then Oona, who was in Montreal had to sign off since the people at her party were starting some white elephant gift game.

Smiling and with a full heart, Triss set her tablet down on the bed and went back out into the main part of the house.

Asher had classic rock playing softly through speakers hidden in the living room and he was humming as he rubbed oil on the baked potatoes.

"Have a good chat with your sister?" he asked, startling her that he knew she was there. She hadn't made a sound. But then again, the man was former military so he could probably hear a mouse fart in the walls.

"I did," she said, sidling up next to him at the counter.

He tilted his head to a decanted bottle of wine. "If you're interested."

"I'm very interested." She grinned and poured herself a glass, then one for him. Bringing the glass to her lips, she studied his profile.

Damn, he was handsome. Strong jaw, long, but not *too* long of a nose. It was a little crooked, like he'd broken it once or twice. He also had that thick white scar on his chin. But that only added to his rugged appeal, if she did say so herself.

His eyes were a deep midnight-blue and the speckles of white reminded her of stars on a twilight sky.

"How'd you like your steak?" he asked, interrupting her ogling.

She had to shake her head and blink a few times. "Sorry?"

Like he knew what she was doing and where her thoughts were wandering, he glanced at her with a smug smile. "How'd you like your *meat*?"

Inside me.

Was that the correct answer?

"Uh ... medium rare, please," she said, licking her lips.

He nodded.

"So uh ... do you have any family around that you are avoiding on Christmas?" Her chuckle was forced, but he seemed open to conversation, and a thousand and one questions hammered at the door in her brain, but she still needed to tread lightly with this stranger. She didn't want him to shut down.

He grunted and drizzled olive oil all over a sheet pan of broccoli florets. "Dad's dead, mom is at her sister's in Missouri. Older siblings, like Hannah's dad, Otis, is in Utah with his new wife and her kids and my older sister, Mary, the oldest of all of us, is where she goes every year for Christmas ..."

"Which is?"

His expression turned sour. "She and a bunch of women from her church go down to impoverished places in Mexico and bring food and toys and stuff to the kids."

"That sounds incredible. Why did you make a face like you just bit into a lemon then?"

"Because she's not doing it for the right reasons. She posts about it all on social media and the way she depicts the people she's helping is wrong. She's exploitative about it, calls their houses 'shanties' and the kids 'grubby little gremlins.' Her posts are like, '*Look at this filthy little thing. His smile lit up my heart when I washed his face and gave him a teddy bear*.'"

Bile coated the back of Triss's tongue.

Asher's face was stony. "There is no altruism about what she's doing. It's all for show and for people to praise her for her good deeds. For her to get into a better level in heaven or some shit."

He had a giant brick of parmesan cheese and began to generously grate it over top of the broccoli florets.

"That sounds horrible," Triss finally said, having to have another sip of her wine to get rid of the bitter taste in her mouth. "At least people are getting food and toys and stuff..."

"Yeah, but at the cost of their dignity as my sister's social media fodder. If I were to do that shit, I wouldn't tell a soul I did it. I wouldn't post about it—not that I have social media because fuck that shit—and I sure as shit wouldn't use them to make myself look better. Nate's on all that insta-snap-tik-book shit, so he tells me she does it. I can't be bothered with any of it." He pressed buttons on the oven so it would preheat, then glanced at her. "Sorry, I get a little hot under the collar when I talk about my sister and her *charity* work. She doesn't do anything out of the goodness of her heart—not a damn thing and it makes me sick."

"Yeah, she sounds like a bit of a monster, to be honest. I take it you're not close?"

"No. She lived mostly with her mother when Nate and I were born. We only saw her on weekends, and she was eighteen, too when I was born. So ... but that didn't stop her from trying to *mom* Nate and I and from day-one. We were not having it though. She actually criticized my mom and how she parented, when Mary didn't have any kids of her own. She does now, and they don't even talk to her."

"So people see her for who she truly is then?"

"Enough that she isn't close with anybody from our side of the family. Is on her third husband and I'm not even sure he likes her."

"Well, who would?"

Asher snorted in agreement. "She tried to use Nate and I and the fact that we're veterans. Tried to spin an angle where she was helping us reacclimate to life in the states. Took pictures of herself bringing us food and carrying welcome home banners and shit."

"NO!"

He nodded. "Yeah. Bitch didn't even come to Colorado when we got home. She pretended she did and posted all this shit from her place in Utah. *So proud of my brothers. Hashtag mybrothersareheros.*"

A cringy shiver shook Triss's body. "Dear God."

"So, to answer your question, my mom who lives here in Denver, is spending Christmas in Missouri, my Dad is dead, sister can go fuck herself and Otis and I are not particularly close, although I'm close with Hannah and her two brothers, Will and Sam."

"Will and Sam are great. Their kids are so stinkin' cute, too." She sipped her wine. "Does your dad have any siblings? Do you have any aunts or uncles?"

He shook his head. "He was a twin, but his brother, Felix, died when they were eighteen. Overdose. Then my dad died a couple of years ago from a heart attack. So now it's just Nate, me, Otis, and Altruism Mary."

Triss snorted. "Ba Humbug?"

That made him smile. "No. I just don't see the point of decorations if there is nobody here to appreciate them. It just makes work. I don't spend enough time in the house to appreciate it. If I had kids and a family it'd be different." He turned to face her, leaning his hip against the counter and showing her all that big sexy chest, arm muscles and thick neck. Hot damn, he was fine. "What about you, Ms. Triss, what's your family story and why aren't you spending the holiday with your sisters and parents?"

Well, that was a loaded question if ever there was one.

She lifted one eyebrow. "How much time do you have?"

Chapter Fifteen

"All night," he said, sipping his wine.

"Where do I begin?" Triss said, blowing out a breath and filling up her glass with more wine.

The timer on the oven beeped to say that it was finished preheating, so Asher put the potatoes in, then turned to her. "We got lots of time before I need to get the meat going, grill is already preheating slowly, so come, let's go sit in the living room."

He took her hand and in his big, calloused one and a flicker of desire ignited in her belly.

They went over to the couch, and to her delight, he pulled her feet into his lap and started to absentmindedly massage them with one hand while holding his wine glass with the other. "So what was life like growing up with four sisters? Does your dad have a golf addiction just so he could escape the hormones?"

She laughed. "Not quite. Pasha is two years older than me. She's a pediatrician, married to this blond behemoth who is also former military but Canadian, and she lives with him and their kids in Canada."

"Navy? Marines? Army? Airforce?" His interest was clearly piqued.

She smiled then groaned when he hit a particularly wonderful spot on the arch of her left foot. "Navy I think, but then special forces. Joint Task Force maybe?"

Asher grunted. "They're good guys."

"Then there's me, and then Mieka who is three years younger than me and this gorgeous dancer who works on cruise ships, dates officers and travels all over the world living the dream."

"Sounds busy and chaotic if you ask me."

"Oh, it's that, too. But I mean she travels everywhere, and parties in the hottest nightclubs all over the world."

"Not my jam, but good for her." He switched to Triss's other foot.

"Mine either, but I am a little jealous about all the travel. I've hardly been anywhere. I went to college right after high school and got my bachelor's, then my master's and I've been working ever since. I've got a bunch of student loans I'm still working to pay off. I can't justify a trip when I owe the bank." She sipped her wine. "Then Oona is four years younger than Mieka and in the final stages of completing her master's in psychology in Montreal. She wants to get her PhD, too, crazy girl."

"And the baby?" he probed, switching to the other foot and pushing his big thumbs into the pad of her big toe. She moaned and her pussy clenched.

"That's Rayma," she said on a blissful sigh. "She's six years younger than Oona. Both she and Oona were actually whoopsie babies."

His dark chocolate-like chuckle wrapped around her like a thick, warm embrace and she made an attempt to snuggle into it if that was possible. "Sounds like your parents missed the safe sex talk."

"And yet they preached abstinence to us girls since we were old enough to understand."

His brows shot up. "Abstinence doesn't work, everybody knows that."

"Well, that's not what my parents thought." She sighed. "I love them, I do. My mom's family were Kosovo refugees who moved to Maryland when she was twelve. Her family kept their heads down and became the ultimate passivists and trouble-duckers. They worked hard, never ruffled feathers. Didn't drink or rubble rouse. They didn't even jaywalk. They were terrified they'd be deported, so they didn't want to draw any unnecessary attention to themselves."

He shook his head, his expression grim and understanding, but he didn't say anything.

"She and my dad met in high school and they kind of brought that passivist, avoid trouble mentality into their own family. But I'd say they took it a step further."

"How so?"

She loved how open he was to talking and how active he listened. She could tell that he was absorbing everything she said and not tuning in and out or nodding just to make her think he heard her. Lorne did that to her all the time and it was infuriating.

Sometimes she'd throw in something obscure like she saw a three-headed giraffe at the library, just to see if he was listening. And when he replied, "That's nice." She knew he wasn't.

Lorne was an ass. Echo could have him.

Asher brought her big toe to his mouth and bit it playfully over her sock. "How so?" he repeated.

She grinned at him. She could easily stay in this spot forever.

"My parents raised my sisters and me like we were guilty of crimes we never even committed. We weren't allowed to go to parties, barely allowed to have playdates, weren't even give the chance to really think for ourselves. We couldn't make messes or get dirty. They didn't believe in trick or treating, didn't have the money to put us all in recreational activities. They don't drink. They're not even religious or anything, they just think alcohol leads to bad decisions and trouble."

"Which it *can*. But sober people can make poor choices, too."

Nodding, she sipped her wine, but ended up finishing it. Asher noticed and swapped their glasses, letting her drink his. "You might be my new favorite person, Asher Harris," she said with a smile before sipping from his wine glass.

All he did was grin.

"While other teens our age went to parties, we were forced to stay home. Only Mieka and Rayma were brave enough to sneak out. Pasha toed the line more than any of us and was the perfect child, leaving nearly impossible shoes to fill. But Oona and I idolized our big sister, so we toed the line most of the time, too. Rayma was the rebel, though. When she was seventeen she got into trouble and my parents—who had never had to deal with a 'reckless child' before—didn't know what to do with her, so they shipped her off to Pasha to reform." She shook her head. "That was the big wake-up call to all of us that our parents were far from perfect and we most definitely did not want to grow up to be like them."

"What kind of shit did Rayma get into?"

She shrugged. "Heavy shit with an outlaw biker gang. It was scary."

Raking his free hand through his hair, he shook his head. "Shit, that's rough."

"Our parents would just say stupid shit to us like, 'What if you want to go into politics and pictures of you drinking and around drugs and at parties surface when you're running?'" She rolled her eyes. "Big fucking whoop. Not one of us has any desire to go into politics, I'll tell you that much."

He snorted. "No? You don't want to become Senator Triss?"

"I'm good, thanks. I'll stick to my day job of effectively changing lives for the better, not just *saying* I'm going to do it, but then actually do dick all."

He tickled her instep. "That's my girl."

Oooh, that comment had her getting warm all over. Or was it the wine? Or was it just being this close to Asher, studying his rugged profile, and having him work those long fingers into her feet like nobody ever had? Maybe all of the above?

"My mom is a very judgmental person. 'Look at those girls and what they're wearing. Their parents have no idea what kind of situation they're sending their daughters in to. Drugs. Alcohol. Boys. Sex. No clue.'" She clucked her tongue like her mother always would, then made her voice go high and nasally as if her mother sounded like Fran Drescher from The Nanny (which she didn't). "I can't believe Ronald and Karen are letting their daughters go out wearing that. Do they even know where the party is? Who is going to be there?"

Triss rolled her eyes and finished Asher's wine glass.

His eyes went wide, and with a knowing, sexy smile, he gently placed her feet on the couch and went to the kitchen. He checked on the potatoes, put the broccoli into the oven, as well and brought the wine decanter back with him, topping up both their glasses.

"Thank you," she said when he handed her freshly poured glass.

"Do that impression of your mother again," he said with a playful smirk.

She wrinkled her nose. "No. But I'll do my dad." She cleared her throat and dropped her voice several octaves. "No kid of mine will ever have a tattoo. Those are for bikers, criminals and gang members. You wouldn't put a bumper sticker on a Ferrari, would you?"

That voice made her voice so scratchy she need more wine.

"But you have a tattoo."

"All five of us have tattoos. We have the matching heart tattoos and then my sisters have other ones, as well. I only have the hearts, but I'm not opposed to others."

"And your parents have no idea?"

"None."

"That's sad."

Sighing, she nodded. "It is, but I don't really know my parents any other way. And I do love them. But for my mental health, I keep my distance. We all do, unfortunately. None of us want to raise our kids the way we were raised. The Mullins across the street knew where their daughters were going. They drove them to the parties and picked them up. And Natasha and Amber were usually wearing skinny jeans, ballet flats, and cardigans over tank tops. Their parents provided them with the proper tools to make the right choices. Our parents just criticized everything and everyone to us trying to convince us—and often succeeding—that their way was the right way and everyone else was wrong and terrible and should be flayed alive." She said this last bit with wide eyes. "Okay, maybe not flayed, but heavily reprimanded until their ears bled."

Chuckling softly, he hauled her into his lap.

"Careful with the wine," she teased, straddling his lap and holding onto her wineglass with one hand while resting her other arm on his broad, sturdy shoulder.

"You want kids one day?" he asked, cradling her waist in his hands and making her feel so safe, not that his lap was a cliff she would suddenly tumble from, but his embrace was solid and reassuring. She knew with Asher there holding her, she was literally and figuratively in good hands.

She giggled. Oh boy, the wine was really hitting her.

"I do," she said with a smile she knew was goofy and wine-induced. "And I hope, that if I do have them, I'll be more sympathetic and attentive if they have dyslexia like me. It was tough growing up the middle of five girls. I definitely didn't get the extra help learning how to read that I needed. A lot of that fell to Pasha."

"I'm sorry you had to deal with that. That must have been tough."

"It was. It's part of what led me to become a speech path, though. I wanted to help kids, *people* with learning difficulties. And I do, and my life is richer for it. What about you, do you want kids?"

His shoulder lifted under her arm. "I figured it would be in the cards eventually. Not against the idea. I'm getting kind of old, so, who knows if it'll actually happen."

"Spoken like a true man who has no idea what he wants."

He chuckled. "Yeah, I guess ..." He glanced at the clock over the mantle. "I need to check the spuds and broc, then probably think about getting the meat on." Holding her hips, he pressed his mouth to hers in a quick but solid kiss that woke up the butterflies in her belly, then like she weighed nothing at all, moved her onto the couch so he could get up.

"Can I help you with anything?" she asked, sipping her wine.

"You can keep your sweet ass on the couch and look pretty," he said, tossing a panty-melting grin over his shoulder at her as he donned an oven mitt with chickens on it and opened the oven.

She took another sip of her wine. "Oh, that I can do."

He served her up the most delicious steak of her life. If she hadn't been so full and quite tipsy from the wine, Triss was certain she would have licked off the juice and remnants of the rub from her plate.

They did the dishes together, then he brought one glass and a bottle of "good bourbon" out to the hot tub with them where they snuggled up naked in the deep lounge section of the tub and stared up at the starry sky.

"Not a bad Christmas," she murmured, accepting the joint from him, putting it between her lips, and filling up her lungs.

She held her breath for a moment, then released the smoke up into the sky, watching it disappear in the ether.

"Yeah?" he grunted. He took the joint from her. "Beats a tree, stockings and turkey with the family?"

"One hundred percent."

Even though they'd had a bit of a rough afternoon, their morning and evening were hands down probably the best Christmas she could remember having in her adult life. At least the most laid back and stress-free she'd had in her life for sure.

He kissed her shoulder.

She leaned her head back against his chest and closed her eyes. "Tell me a story from your childhood. A good one, a memory you reflect fondly on and often. Maybe one of you and your uncle and you and Nate on his ranch."

He was quiet for a moment, but she could tell by the way his chest moved that he was taking a hit off the joint. "One time, Nate and I were staying with our Uncle Tom—he's our mom's brother—and Nate thought it would be a cool idea to stand on the back of two goats, like they were water skis and make the goats walk and eventually run."

"Dear God, I hope you talked him out of it, or at least got a video."

He snorted a laugh. "I didn't and I did. He stupidly used rope, which he tied around the goats' bellies and then made me tie over his feet so they were secure. More rope went around their horns so that he had something to hold on to. Then he told me to open the barn door. I did as I was told and my brother ripped his pants, tore his groin muscle, and cried harder and longer than I ever saw him—or another person—to this day."

Even though she was only hearing the story, the thought of that happening had Triss crossing her legs where she sat and grimacing from empathized pain. "And what did your uncle have to say about things?"

"He said that what happened to Nate was punishment enough, and if there was a God, he'd have taken care of that idiot ever procreating right then and there."

Triss giggled. "Oh man, I bet you two got up to a lot of mischief as boys."

"More than I can even remember. I have scars that I couldn't even begin to tell you where they came from, but I know they came from doing something stupid and dangerous. Like the time Nate convinced me to piss on an electric fence. No scars, but the memory is vivid."

"Oh my God. But you also probably have a lot of great memories, right?"

"Yeah ..." His tone was nostalgic and she didn't have to see him to know he was smiling, she could hear it in his voice.

Would he look back on their time together fondly? Or would she end up being a "scar" on his memories that he didn't remember getting?

As attentive as he could be, she still struggled to read the guy and where his head was with everything, particularly what *they* were.

Yes, she kept telling herself this was just a short-lived snowy fling, but her heart kept telling her otherwise. Her heart, which had picked itself up and Kintsugied itself back together rather quickly after Lorne, was telling her that Asher was more than just a fling and that what they had going on was real and worth exploring.

He passed her the joint and she took another hit, letting the smoke make the worry in her brain blurry and soften all those sharp, jagged questions that kept poking her and distracting her. She shouldn't be fretting about any of that now. She just needed to live in the moment. Enjoy the moment. Enjoy Asher.

"What's say we head to bed and Santa can come down my chimney," she said, reaching over and snuffing out the finished joint in the ashtray. Then she grabbed the lowball of bourbon and finished that, too.

Asher's chuckle was pure sex. "I don't necessarily know what that means, but I can take a guess. I like the way you think, Mrs. Claus." Then he scooped her up, making her squeal and proceed to yell, 'Ho-ho-ho', all the way up to bedroom where he tossed her to the bed and made *her* come down the chimney several times that night.

Chapter Sixteen

It was December twenty-seventh and Asher was avoiding asking Triss when she planned to leave because to be brutally honest, he just wasn't ready to let her go. So he avoided asking if she'd checked out flights, or if she'd noticed if the plow had gone down the road. Because he didn't care.

If he could keep her until the new year—and after—he gladly would.

She wasn't a burden or an inconvenience, in fact, she was a breath of fresh air, a capable set of extra hands and a damn good woman to have curled up in his arms at night.

But every time she would go back to "her room" to get her tablet, he would brace himself for the revelation that she'd booked her flights and would be leaving the next day. He'd been doing this since Christmas when she went to speak to her sister. And then on the twenty-sixth when she spoke to her other sister and her parents.

However, each time, he breathed a sigh of relief that she hadn't booked a flight and would be staying with him another night.

How could he tell her that this was more than just a fling when their worlds were so different, their lives were on opposite sides of the country, and his head so fucked up? She didn't deserve to take on his mess of a brain and all the triggers that came with it.

She had a life in Connecticut, a thriving career and he was sure by this time next year she'd have a new boyfriend and big sparkly rock on her finger.

Any man that got to spend even a moment with Triss would be stupid not to snap her up and pop the question. She was brilliant, beautiful, and ballsy. A winning combination in his book.

A sexy groan from the other side of the bed had him glancing over at the naked woman stirring beside him.

He'd been awake for about twenty minutes, staring despondently up at the ceiling. He thought about ducking under the covers and waking her up the way he had on Christmas and yesterday, his cock certainly wanted him to, but he didn't.

His brain wasn't there.

His brain was on Triss and the fact that at some point, she would leave.

She would leave him.

And that made his chest hurt more than he could ever admit.

How did a woman get so under his skin so damn fast? And so damn deep?

It didn't make any sense.

Her warm, soft hand slid across his chest and she curled into his side. "'Morning, cowboy," she said sleepily, not bothering to open her eyes.

"Rancher." He had his arms behind his head, but he released one and wrapped it around her, stroking her hipbone with his thumb. "And morning."

"How long have you been awake?"

"Not long."

She moaned again and snuggled in deeper. "I could stay in here, warm and cozy, forever," she murmured, pressing a kiss to his chest. "You're like a big, muscly furnace."

He smiled. Yeah, he could stay right where they were forever, too.

"But Fumble will rebel and pick the lock on all the stalls and before we know it, we'll look up from our little nest and there will be a barn full of animals staring at us from the bedroom window."

He chuckled. "I would not put it past Fumble to do something like that. But he'd probably take it a step further and break into the house and lead all the animals up the stairs to stare at us in bed."

"Oh, if Macklin saw you in bed with me, he'd probably have a conniption." She giggled.

"Oh, the old boy is definitely crushing. He's even been giving me the stink-eye if I get to close to you out in the barn."

"Dare's your horse, right?"

"Yeah. And Umber is Nate's."

"How long have you had Dare?"

"Since we bought the ranch, so almost six years. We bought Dare and Umber at the same time, then Macklin and Greenleigh a year later."

"And the herd just grew after that?"

He laughed. "Yep. The herd just grew after that."

She kissed his chest again. "We should probably go feed that herd, though, huh? Before they get any ideas about escaping."

With a weary sigh, he nodded. "Yeah, we probably should. I don't normally sleep in like this, so they're probably already formulating a plan, or at the very least organizing a search party. Or a coup."

Her tinkling laugh caused warmth and contentment to seep through him, so with a growl, he rolled on top of her, pinning her beneath his body, and cradling her face in his hands. He brushed the hair away, gently off her cheeks, staring down into those warm, golden-brown eyes.

She blinked back at him and smiled, looping her arms around his neck and spreading her legs so he could settle between them.

More heat, more contentment spun through him, to the point where it almost made him lightheaded. Was this love?

So soon?

So quickly?

"Maybe the herd can wait ten more minutes?" she asked, lifting her hips up so that he was notched at her hot, wet center.

He tipped his hips and gently slid inside her. "I think they could probably wait fifteen." Then he took his woman, because even if it was only temporarily, Triss was his. And he was going to make the most of the time they had left. Claim her as much as he could, so that when she left, he was branded on her mind. Because she was certainly branded on his heart.

Triss pressed a kiss to Mercy's nose after putting him back in his stall and the big lug swung his head over the opening. "You be good, Mr. Mercy," she said scratching his ears. He head-butted her gently, asking for my scratches and she laughed. "Now you're just trying to rub it into Macklin's face." She peered down the barn and sure enough, Macklin was watching them.

Asher appeared from where he'd been out with the chickens. "Lunch?"

She nodded. "Sounds good. My belly is rumbling."

"Head on in and get cleaned up and I'll join you in a moment."

She did as she was told, making sure to give a little bit of love to each horse she passed before finally making her exit.

It'd froze hard last night since it had been so clear, but at least it hadn't snowed anymore.

There were some gray clouds off to the north, though, that looked like they had snow in them, so she wasn't holding her breath that this was the last of the white stuff for a while.

Stomping the snow off her boots as she climbed the steps to the front door, she peered down the long driveway toward the road, where sure enough, a plow was finally making its merry way.

"About damn time," she muttered, watching it for another few moments.

Asher had kept the driveway plowed and cleared, but he wasn't going to tackle the road, so even though she could get down to the road if she needed to, no cab or otherwise would dare drive out here to get her.

She'd been looking at flights nearly every day on her tablet, but hadn't yet booked one because the weather was unpredictable and with the roads not cleared she didn't want to book something but not be able to get to the airport for her flight.

Plus, she was perfectly content where she was.

The house was warm and cozy, the company was sexy, muscly, and good in bed, and she had two horses—Mercy and Macklin—fighting over her affections. Did life really get any better?

She hung up her coat, knit cap and gloves, then toed out of her boots, leaving them to dry by the front door.

The wood stove was still fogging away, so the house was delightfully warm and inviting.

She'd made quesadillas with cheese, chicken, and black beans for lunch yesterday, but today she was feeling like something a little different.

Digging through Asher's pantry and freezer, she found an unopened jar of pesto and a small bag of already peeled shrimp, as well as some English muffins.

Mmm ... pesto shrimp melts sounded like the perfect kind of lunch.

She was busy with lunch prep when she heard Asher come in.

Peeling carrots for carrot sticks with ranch dip, she stood over the sink but smiled when he wrapped his arms around her waist and kissed the side of her neck.

"Go wash up. Lunch is almost ready."

He nipped her neck then disappeared.

She turned the oven over to broil so that the pesto shrimp melts could get a nice crispy cheesy crust on top, then turned back to her carrots.

Asher returned smelling of soap and straw. "Do we have time for a quick ..." He pushed his pelvis against her butt. "Before lunch?"

She chuckled, set the peeler and carrot down on the counter, then spun to face him, looping her arms around his neck. "Are all cowboys this insatiable."

"Rancher. And I have no idea. Never slept with one myself. And I'm not normally," he said, dropping his mouth to the side of her throat and pressing warm, open-mouthed kisses. "You bring out the beast in me." His growl sent shivers rippling through her.

Lifting his head, he took her mouth, plunging his tongue inside and swirling it around until she was lightheaded, warm and with jelly legs.

Pinning her between his hard body and the counter, he gripped her hair and tilted her head up so he could better ravish her mouth. Of course, she let him.

She would let this man do anything to her that brought her pleasure—and maybe even a bit of pain.

They kissed and kissed and kissed. She couldn't get enough.

She knew by the way he pressed his erection against her belly that he could easily take it further, and a big part of her wanted to, too. But they needed to have lunch first.

And at that thought, she remembered the melts.

"Oh shit!" she cried, peeling herself away from him and rushing to the oven. Throwing on the chicken-covered oven mitt, she opened the oven door only to be met with a thick, billowing smoke that hit her in the face.

Immediately, the smoke detector started to wail.

She turned off the broiler and pulled out the tray with the charred remains of their lunch. Shit.

"What the fuck!" Asher roared. His hands over his ears. "What the fuck?"

He was pacing the kitchen, his eyes wild, nostrils flaring as the smoke alarm continued to scream.

"How could you be so stupid? So fucking stupid!"

Opening the door to the laundry room, she stepped inside, then opened the door to the backyard that led to the hot tub. "Out!" she ordered him.

Glaring at her, he did as he was told, while she grabbed a kitchen chair, stood on it and started to wave the oven mitt in front of the smoke alarm to try to get it to turn off.

It took a while since the room was really smokey, but eventually, silence reigned once again and she let out a deep exhale in relief.

After climbing down from the chair, Triss then proceeded to open the window in the kitchen over the sink, a window in the living room, and even the front door just to let the smoke filter out.

With sadness, she dumped the black crumbly shrimp and pesto melt in the trashcan. So much for that brilliant idea.

She tugged a sweater over her black T-shirt since it was still below freezing outside and now she was letting all that cold air in.

"Asher," she called through the open door out to the backyard. "Crisis averted. You can come back in now."

He must be out there in his socks, since like her, he'd probably ditched his snow-covered boots by the front door. And he hadn't been in more than a red-checkered flannel shirt from what she remembered. He was probably freezing.

There was no sign of him though.

Dashing back into the house, she proceeded to close all the windows and doors again, grabbed her jacket and her boots, along with his jacket, then walked through the house to the laundry room and out into the backyard.

Maybe he just jumped into the hot tub to keep warm. That's what she would have done if she'd run out in her socks and nothing but a shirt and jeans.

"Asher?"

There was no sign of him. The hot tub was still closed.

But it wasn't that difficult to follow the tracks in the snow to a small potting shed near the back corner of the yard.

What had he been thinking walking all the way through the snow in his socks? His feet were probably turning blue.

She raced back into the house, grabbed his boots, too, then trudged through

141

the snow toward the shed.

The door was open a crack, so carefully, not wanting to spook him, she opened it.

He was sitting on an overturned bucket, his hands to the side of his head and he was rocking back and forth while resting his elbows on his knees.

Her chest tightened.

What had he gone through? What did he see to trigger him like this?

"Here," she said softly, setting his boots down in front of his feet, then stepping into the freezing shed and draping his jacket around his shoulders. "Come back in when you're ready."

"I'm not coming in until you're gone," he said, not bothering to lift his head, let alone look at her.

"What?" She shook her head. Did she hear him correctly?

"Plow came through. Driveway is clear. You should go. Call a cab, book a flight and go."

Crouching down in front of him, she pressed her hand to his arm, gently. "Asher ... I'm not mad about what happened. It was an accident. I'm sorry if it trigger—"

He lifted his head and glared at her. "It was stupid and irresponsible and you could have burned down the entire fucking house." His voice dripped with acid, sending ice streaking through her veins.

Something big and scary trembled inside of her and she sucked in a sharp breath. "It was *an accident*. You were distracting me, but I'm not *blaming* you for it. These things happen, that's why there are smoke alarms and fire extinguishers, not that I needed one."

His head shook and he dropped his gaze back to the floor. "I think it's best if you just go. I can't predict the next time you're going to *have an accident* and make a noise that triggers me. I just ... you need to go. I'm not ..." His shoulders slumped. "I'm not well. Not in the head anyway. I'm fucking broken. This was a fling and nothing more. You need to leave. Now."

142

Her heart hurt for her cowboy

With her chin trembling and throat full of spikes, she stood back up. She didn't want to go. Didn't want to leave him, but she wasn't sure what else to do.

She could wait him out, hope he returned to the house and they could talk things through, or she could do as he asked and just leave.

She wasn't his to fix. He'd made that clear.

Clenching her jaw to keep her emotions in check, at least until she got away from him, she nodded. "All right. I've obviously over-stayed my welcome. I will call a cab and be gone within half an hour. Thank you for your hospitality. I appreciate you letting me stay here. It was nice meeting you."

She waited for him to lift his head and look at her, but he didn't.

But she also wasn't going to leave without saying her piece. Without clearing her conscience and doing what she could—a last ditch effort—to let him know how she felt. "You're not broken, you know. And even if you were, that doesn't mean you can't put the pieces that remain back together. Most of us are a variation of a Kintsugi bowl. Cracked and damaged, but with a little patience, some lacquer, and gold dust we can still be beautiful and useful. We're not defined by our flaws and painful past, but it is a part of who we are, a part of our structure, and what makes us uniquely us. And I believe it's the same with you. You are *not* your trauma or your triggers. You are not broken."

She waited for him to respond, to even look at her, but when she got nothing, not even a shrug, she turned and left, closing the door behind her just as the first tear slid down her cheek.

Chapter Seventeen

God, he was a fucking idiot.

To think that he deserved an amazing woman like Triss given how broken he was, it was honestly laughable.

And the only way he knew he could get her to leave was to push her away. So he'd done that and hated every second of it. His gut spun, his ears buzzed and his heart hurt as he forced out the words and told her to leave. To call a cab, book a flight and go.

But she didn't deserve to deal with his shit. It wasn't her job to fix him.

And he was the kind of broken that you just couldn't fix anyway.

With his teeth chattering and his toes probably frost-bitten, he stayed in the shed until he heard a cab pull up in the driveway in front of the house. Then he waited until he knew that cab would be gone before he gathered his wits—or what was left of them—and his sorry ass and headed back into the house.

The place was cold, dull and lifeless and he knew precisely why.

Because Triss wasn't there.

She was gone.

Anger clawed sharp talons in his throat making it difficult to swallow. He was developing a headache, his molars were so tightly clenched and as a form of punishment to himself, he didn't bother fixing himself anything for lunch.

He didn't really have an appetite anymore anyway.

He put on fresh, warm socks, and a sweater, then shoved his feet back into his boots and tossed on his coat. He was about to head back to the barn to go and get Macklin and Mercy's wrath over with when he told them Triss left, when his phone started to warble in his pocket.

He put it to his ear. "Hey bro," Nate said. "We just stopped to get gas, we're about three hours out, so we'll see you soon unless another snowstorm hits."

"Don't even fucking joke about that," Asher grumbled.

"Where's Triss, I want to talk to her," Hannah said. "If she's sucking your dick, never mind though."

"Tell our niece to show her uncle some fucking respect," Asher said to his brother, every word hurt to get out. And at the mention of Triss, a sharp spike of regret lodged itself in his chest, dead-center and he could already tell it wasn't going anywhere.

"Asher says that they're taking a break," Nate replied to Hannah, a smile in his voice.

"She's not here."

"Where is she?" Nate asked.

"Left."

"To town for more condoms?"

"No. Home."

"What the fuck?" Hannah exclaimed. "Let me talk to him. I told him to hump away her heartbreak, not break her heart even more. Give me the phone, Nate."

"Hannah, stop it. Let go."

"Give me the phone."

A commotion ensued on the other end for a moment, then the sound of a truck door slamming echoed through. "She can't get to me out here, the brat," Nate said with a chuckle. "Now, what do you mean Triss is gone?"

"She left. We parted ways. The fling is over."

"Yeah, you definitely sound like a man who was done with her." Asher could just picture his brother shoving his fingers into his hair. "Fuck, bro, what'd you do?"

"A lot of things," Asher said on a sigh.

"I bet. Listen, I'm sorry it ended that way, I really am."

"Yeah, me, too."

"But on another note, I think I might have figured out why Mercy reacts to you the way he does. Do you remember when we first got him, there was a loud noise in the barn, one of the ranch hands dropped something. You reacted like an asshole and tore a strip off Donald like you're prone to do when triggered by a loud noise. We'd only had Mercy a few hours at that point."

Asher's mouth dropped open. The exact same thing happened when Triss knocked over the bucket. He overreacted, triggered by the noise and then the noise and Asher's overreaction sent Mercy into a tailspin.

Was that why Mercy was so antsy around him?

"I went back and watched the barn feed from when we first got Mercy, that's where I got that idea," Nate said, cutting through the cannoning thoughts in Asher's head and drawing him back to the present. "I mean, it makes sense, right?"

Yeah, it made a fuck-ton of sense.

Asher grunted.

"Anyway, bro, we can talk more about it when I'm home, come up with a solution. I mean if Mercy is just a pain in the ass it might be easier to cut our losses and sell him." He made a regretful noise in his throat. "As much as I'd rather not. Was hoping to have him sire foals with a couple of our mares at least. Would like to sell his spunk, too."

"Yeah, I know ..." Asher murmured. "We'll figure something out. Not ready to give up on him yet."

"That's the spirt."

146

Honk! Honk! Honk!

"Would you knock that off?" Nate barked at their niece who was obviously growing impatient in the truck and making it known in a loud and obnoxious way. "I'll see you when we get home. Don't do anything stupid until I get there, okay?"

"Can't make that promise. You know me better than that."

"Yeah," Nate said reluctantly. "I do."

They said their goodbyes and Asher stowed his phone in his back pocket.

He should chase after her.

Drive to the airport and make her follow him back to the ranch. Drag her if he had to, just so he could throw her into the bed and spend all night apologizing.

But she didn't deserve a man as hot and cold as he was. As easily triggered and broken. Because something else would trigger him eventually and he'd lose his shit all over again. It was inevitable. And a person as sweet and pure as Triss didn't need to be tangled up with a shadow of a man like Asher.

She was better off in every way. But she'd said a lot of things that made sense and as much as she said he wasn't broken, or that even broken he wasn't useless, he was having a hard time believing it.

What'd she call him? A Kintsugi bowl?

Yeah, he didn't believe that. He was broken and there was no fixing him, no filling in the cracks with lacquer and gold dust. And it sure as hell wasn't her job to try and piece him back together. He didn't want to lay that responsibility on anybody, not even himself, which was why at forty-two he was still a fucking mess of a human being who only got along with horses.

Glancing out the window, he watched the fat fluffy flakes fall.

He hadn't ridden the fence since that first day with Triss, he needed to do it. Those hillbilly assholes had probably torn through his fence again and done donuts with their snowmobiles. Motherfuckers.

Nate wanted to electrify the fence, and up until now Asher had been reluctant to do it, now he was thinking it wasn't such a bad idea and they might need to factor that into the coming year's budget.

He headed out to the barn, saddled up Dare, then the two of them took off. It was closing in on three o'clock, so he'd have to be quick, otherwise, they might get caught in the dark and he definitely didn't want to be riding in the snow and freezing cold in the dark.

The wind picked up a quarter of the way into their ride, hitting them hard in the face. Asher had to pull the buff he wore around his neck up over his nose and mouth, so just his eyes peeked out, otherwise, he'd be sure to get frostbite before he reached the barn.

Dare was slow-moving as the snow was now up to the horse's knees, but he was a good horse and powered forward. Asher leaned down and patted his neck. "Doing good, buddy. I'm sorry about this. I'll give you extra treats and a warm blanket when we get back."

Even though it was snowing, the divots and snowmobile tracks up ahead were visible. As was the cut fence.

Motherfuckers!

"Fuck," he murmured, tightening his hold on Dare's reins. "Stupid assholes." He guided Dare closer, but the horse must have found a gopher hole and with a loud cry, Dare's knee buckled and he went down sideways, taking Asher with him.

They crashed into the barbed wire fencing and Dare screamed even louder, thrashing and crying, trying to get up but all the while crushing and pinning Asher beneath him, and grinding Asher deeper into the snow and wire.

The wire dug into and cut up his coat and jeans, piercing his skin where his coat rode up exposing his back.

Dare continued to flail, now the two of them were a tangled mess of wire. Dare was bleeding and scratched up and every time he tried to get up, he'd scream in agony and put more of his weight on Asher.

"It's okay, buddy." Asher said, wincing from the pain and weight of the horse on him. "It's okay. Shhhh."

Dare's nostrils flared as he breathed heavily. His heart was pounding and his chest heaved.

Asher checked his toes by trying to wiggle them, it seemed like both legs still worked. But for how long? And just because he *thought* he was moving his toes didn't mean he was.

Releasing the reins, he shoved his hands into the snow, attempting to find his phone which he's stupidly put in his back pocket. He knew better than to keep it there when he rode, in case it got bounced out. He normally put it in his coat pocket to keep it safe and dry. He was just so distracted with Triss leaving and what Nate said about Mercy.

His heart hurt, his brain hurt and now his legs and back fucking hurt, too. Not a damn part of him wasn't in pain.

Mercy. That damn horse. Here he'd been calling Mercy an asshole when really, it was Asher that was the asshole and Mercy was just a horse that didn't trust Asher because he was unpredictable, which was entirely true.

It made so much fucking sense now that he thought about it.

And if he really thought about it, he was sure there was probably at least one if not two more times where he probably yelled or lashed out around Mercy, which of course would cause the horse to have an aversion to him. It was a wonder more of the horses didn't go squirrely around Asher.

Dare tried to get up again, but that only crushed Asher more and the horse let out another scream.

The more Dare tried to move, the more tangled they became.

He found his phone in his pocket, thank fuck, and fumbled to drag it out from under him, but it wasn't easy. Dare was six hundred pounds of American Standardbred muscle.

Despite wearing gloves, Asher's fingers were stiff as he attempted to wrap them around his phone, but Dare's struggling kept causing him to lose his grip on the phone.

"Shh, Dare. Shh, buddy. I know. I know it hurts. I know it's scary and cold, but we need to stay calm, otherwise we're both seriously fucked."

This was why he and Nate spent a large part of their spring and summer laying on their bellies in the field dressed in their camo gear and shooting fucking prairie dogs and gophers. Those little bastards dug holes all over the fields, then Asher's horses stepped in one and it was a motherfucking shit show. They'd lost three beautiful horses over the last couple of years to broken legs from those fucking holes.

Well, this coming summer he was going to increase his hunting schedule. He'd take out every little hole-digging bastard until the species were all extinct if he had to.

Dare was still breathing heavy, but he'd stopped moving.

The thought of having to put Dare out of his misery burned a hot insidious trail through Asher until bile coated the back of his tongue and he thought he might puke.

"Shhh," Asher said, freeing his hand from beneath the horse and stroking Dare's neck. "Shhh. It's okay, buddy. It's okay."

He attempted to get his phone again, and finally managed to snag it, but when he brought it up to his face and tried to turn it on, it wouldn't.

It must have gotten water-logged from the snow or run out of battery or something.

"Fuck," he growled, keeping his voice low, so as to not scare Dare.

Dare panted and Asher closed his eyes.

It was starting to get dark.

How could he have been so stupid as to start riding the fence this close to dusk and in the fucking wind and snow?

Because he wasn't thinking clearly, that was why. He was only thinking of Triss and how he'd stupidly let her go. How he'd stupidly *told* her to go.

He'd been so worried about scaring her away when she finally saw how truly broken he was, that he sent her away first. Idiot. If he went on the offensive, less people would get hurt. It was a mantra he'd been telling himself for years. Only he wasn't warding off evil spirits, he was warding off good, decent people and the real evil spirits were the dark shadows of his heart and mind. The parts of him desperate to be rid of anybody who cared about him before they uncovered his faults and he tripped over them as he scrambled to collect them, falling face-first into more heartache. If he sought out those shadowy demons, if he predicted them before they arrived, they couldn't get to him first, right?

Only now those demons had gone and chased away one of the most beautiful, brightest angels of hope and love and light that he'd ever encountered, all because he was scared. Scared of being loved, broken pieces and all. Because what if those broken pieces just weren't enough? What if those broken pieces were jagged and hurt someone? Hurt Triss. What if he couldn't give her what she needed, what she deserved, because he wasn't whole enough inside to do it?

Swallowing, he let his muscles relax beneath the weight of the horse and stared up at the sky, the falling flakes mesmerizing, like one of those 3D pictures you have to stare at for a while before the image hidden inside reveals itself.

No matter how hard he tried, though, the only image he kept seeing was Triss. Standing there with her sassy smile, challenging him, forcing him to look deep inside himself to a place he'd avoided going since retiring from active duty.

A place he wasn't sure he had the strength to return to.

"We just gotta ... keep warm, Dare. Buddy, just keep warm. It's okay. We'll be okay. Nate and Hannah will get here and they'll come looking for us. You'll see. It'll all ... be ... okay."

A shiver wracked through him and his teeth began to chatter.

He patted Dare on the neck. "We got this, buddy. Just ... stay calm. We'll figure a way out of this ... I promise."

Darkness was closing in, but the snow wasn't letting up. Dare was still warm enough that the flakes melted the moment it touched his body, but that wouldn't last forever.

Asher blinked away the flurries and wiped his eyes. He turned his head and tugged his jacket hood over his head as best he could.

He was cold.

Really cold and he was starting to get tired.

Maybe he just needed to sleep for a bit. Then he wouldn't feel the cold so much if he was asleep. And when he woke up, Nate and Hannah would be there and Nate could help him get Dare back to the barn.

Yeah, he just needed to close his eyes for a bit.

Blinking, he gave his head a violent shake, which caused Dare to stir and push more of his weight on Asher.

What was he thinking? He couldn't fall asleep.

Sleep in the cold meant death. It meant he was succumbing to hypothermia.

With trembling fingers, he checked his phone again to see if it'd just gotten a bit water-logged and had decided to start working again.

No such luck.

A black screen met him and he silently cursed his decision to not get one of those LifeProof cases that Nate had. Well, if he made it out of this situation alive, he'd sure as fuck be buying one of those cases. Along with an electrical fence. He'd go to counseling, too, to help with his PTSD, maybe the veteran's center again. He'd gone once or twice with Nate, but stopped when things at the ranch started to get busier. But he'd start going again, he'd make it a priority.

He'd also fly out to Connecticut, find Triss and apologize for being so fucking stupid. Even though he didn't deserve her, he did deserve happiness and she was the definition of happiness. Light, grace, brilliance and beauty. She brought it all into his dark and dismal existence and he'd foolishly sent her away thinking it was for the better.

Fuck, even if she slammed the door in his face, at least he'd know he tried. Hopefully, she wouldn't slam the door until he apologized, because she definitely deserved that. She deserved to have her fucking feet kissed and every wish she ever dreamed to be granted.

Yeah, if he got out of this alive, he was going to find Triss and if she'd let him, never let her fucking go.

"We got this, Dare," he mumbled, his teeth chattering even more. "Just hold on a little longer."

Dare's breathing had evened out, but his body was starting to tremble. Either he was going into shock, and/or, he was starting to catch hypothermia.

Asher's eyes closed and he patted Dare again. "It's okay, buddy."

At least, he hoped it would be.

Chapter Eighteen

They'd been driving for twenty-five minutes, the tears in Triss's eyes fat blobs that obscured her vision and made hot tracks down her cheeks as she stared despondently out the window of the cab, her body wracked with silent sobs.

She knew Asher was hurting and that he didn't mean the things he said to her. She knew it the first time he'd been triggered and lashed out. But she'd made him apologize that time so he knew he couldn't get away with that shit, and that she wasn't somebody who would allow themselves to be spoken to like that.

This time, she figured he'd know to apologize, and then everything would be okay.

But that hadn't happened.

He let his grief, his trauma and his pain cloud his reasoning and he responded rashly, ordering her to go, blaming her for the smoke detector and burned food.

It had been both their faults, she knew that.

She forgot she had something under the broiler and he had distracted her.

How was Hannah going to react to all of this? Would she tear off several strips from Asher, until she hit bone? Flay him with her words for breaking her best friend's heart?

Probably.

Because as much as Triss didn't want to admit it, given how fast it'd all happened, she'd fallen hard for the troubled rancher and her heart was broken. Probably even more than it had been when she arrived on his doorstep a week ago after Lorne dumped her, ending their three-year relationship.

She chuckled painfully through the tears. She was more upset and heart-broken over a six-day tryst than she was a three-year relationship where she and Lorne lived together, owned a couch together and shared a Netflix account.

Triss already knew that water was thicker than blood in this case and Hannah would side with Triss over Asher. Not that she truly needed to pick a side, but Hannah was all about the hoes before bros.

She was a lot like Rayma. Neither woman had very in-tact filters. They tended to just say what they wanted, fuck the consequences.

In some ways, Triss admired them for that, but in other ways it made her cringe. But what she loved most about both of them was just how hard they loved.

Both Rayma and Hannah were amazing people with the strongest sense of loyalty Triss had ever encountered. And even though their big mouths and lack of filters tended to get them into hot water once in a while, it was their enormous hearts that got them out of that hot water and made Triss grateful to have them in her life.

She was grateful to have Asher in her life, too.

Even though his exterior was tough, weathered and nearly impenetrable, he'd let her see that softer center. Let her experience that gentle heart and goodness that he harbored beneath his armor for the horses and what she already knew to be very few people.

He was a Kintsugi bowl. They both were. Cracked, but not broken. Not enough to be tossed away. Not helpless. Not hopeless.

And she'd regret it for the rest of her life if she didn't fight for what she was sure they had. Not just a fling, not just a tryst, but something real and raw and that could go the distance if they just put in a little work. And maybe a sprinkle of gold dust.

Leaning forward in her seat, she wiped her tears from her cheeks. "I'm really sorry, but could you turn around?"

"Did you forget something?" the driver asked.

She nodded. "I did. And I don't expect you to drive me back to Denver. I actually don't think I'm going to make my flight." She beamed as he slowed the cab down and turned around.

Dusk was starting to settle in, so hopefully that meant Asher was in the house and after a few words and promises they could tumble into bed where she could demand he apologize for being so stupid as to send her away.

The man was very good at apologizing.

Hauling her suitcase back up the front steps of the house, she waved the cab driver off and watched him drive away.

She didn't even bother to knock and just opened the front door and stepped in. "Asher!"

Several heartbeats and tension-filled moments passed, but she already knew he wasn't in the house. She couldn't feel his large presence.

Was he still in the shed?

Has he fallen asleep out there?

Not bothering to remove her boots, she left her suitcase in the foyer and ran through the house, throwing open the door from the laundry room and running through the snow and the falling flakes to the shed. God, if he'd fallen asleep in the cold he could catch hypothermia and die.

She flung open the door and heaved a sigh of relief when he wasn't there still sitting on the bucket.

Was he in the barn?

She didn't bother to go back through the house, since she'd closed all the doors and took the side gate to get to the front yard. From there, she ran across the snow-covered gravel to the barn. "Asher?" She called out. "Asher?"

She scanned the stalls and that's when she noticed that Dare was missing, so was his saddle, bridle and halter.

Shit.

He'd gone out to ride the fence.

And he wasn't back yet.

Worry and panic quivered inside her as she ran back to the house. She grabbed Asher's truck keys from the hook they hung on in the entryway, then ran out to his truck.

She wasn't a good enough rider to brave taking a horse out into this mess. Besides, if she did find Asher and Dare and they were in trouble, how did she expect to get them back if she was on Macklin or Hula-Hoop?

No, a truck made the most amount of sense.

One length of the fence, the fence they'd encountered the biggest hole from the snowmobile riding hillbillies ran parallel to the road. She'd drive the road and see if she could spot them through the bare trees. That was the practical thing to do.

If she couldn't find them, then she'd break through the fence with the truck and drive through the field until she did.

With her plan in place, she turned over the ignition, didn't even bother for the truck to warm up, then peeled off down the driveway.

Once she reached the road, she rolled down her window and using a flashlight she found in the glove box, shone it through the trees to the fence. "Asher!" she called out. "Asher!" She stopped the truck and moved the flashlight through the tree line. "Asher!"

Nothing.

Dread curled through her.

She had a bad feeling about this. A really bad feeling.

Pressing her foot to the accelerator again, she slowly crept along the wrong side of the road, continuing to shine the light through the trees. She reached the opening where the hillbillies on their snowmobiles had to be getting through and stopped again.

"ASHER!" she cried out into the dark, shining her light. "ASHER!"

Movement.

"Triss!" It was faint, but it was there. On the wind. "Triss!" The wind didn't say her name twice. It couldn't. That was Asher. He was out there and he was in trouble.

Oh God!

She took the clearing that led to the fence, driving through the newly cut wire. Snow crunched under her tires, so she had to put it into four-wheel drive. She turned the truck to the left and her heart leaped into her throat when the headlights of the truck landed on Dare on his side, tangled in the barbed wire of the fence. She couldn't see Asher, though.

Climbing out of the truck, but leaving it running, she slogged her way through the snow, panic rippling through her in nauseating waves.

"Triss!" Asher said again, his voice hoarse and low. But she heard it.

She made her way around Dare who blinked up at her with wild, terrified eyes. "Shhh," she said, petting the horse's neck. "It's okay, buddy." Dare's nostrils flared.

Then she found Asher, pinned beneath his horse.

"Oh God, Asher! Oh God, are you okay?"

He smiled sleepily up at her, his lips blue. The buff he'd worn the last time they rode the fence had slid off his face and he probably didn't have the energy to pull it back over. His nose was bright red, so were his cheeks.

She checked his pulse. It was slow, but it was steady.

She needed to get him into the truck and get him warm.

"You came back," he said, his blue lips wobbling.

"I came back to tell you how big of an idiot you are," she said, her chuckle forced. "And that I'm not giving up on what I think we both know is more than just a fling."

He nodded. "More than a fling."

"Can you move your legs?"

"I'm sorry I sent you away. I shouldn't have. You're the best thing that's ever ... happened ... to me."

"Asher, you need to conserve your energy. No unnecessary talking, okay? Can you move your legs?"

He shook his head. "They're frozen."

"They're not frozen. If anything, Dare's body heat has kept them from freezing. But they might be broken. He's a big boy."

She scanned the situation.

When she found the flashlight in the glove box, she saw a number of other tools in there, too. Like bolt cutters and wire cutters. There was also a shovel behind the passenger seat.

Leaning down, she pressed her lips to his, they were ice-cold. "I'll be right back. Okay? I'm going to get you out of this. Both of you. This isn't your ending, I swear it."

All he did was smile and close his eyes.

She pulled the buff back over his mouth and nose, then ran to the truck.

Just as she heaved open the back passenger door, her phone started to ring in her back pocket.

She glanced at it and it was Hannah.

"Hannah!" she exclaimed, answering the phone and balancing it between her cheek and shoulder as she grabbed the shovel and wire cutters. "Where are you?"

"Like twenty minutes from the house. Tell me you're not in the Denver airport heading home. My uncle is an idiot."

"Agreed and I'm not. I came back but Asher wasn't at the house. He went and rode the fence, Dare fell and now Asher is trapped under Dare and they're tangled in the fence wire. I'm here trying to dig him out."

She heard Nate curse in the background.

"We're twenty minutes away," Hannah repeated. "Where in the field are you?"

"Where those hillbilly motherfuckers keep cutting the fence to do donuts in the field."

"Got it," Hannah said. "We're on our way. And Triss?"

"Yeah?" Triss said, making her way back to Asher and Dare.

"I'm glad you didn't give up on him."

"Me, too," she said.

She disconnected the call and shoved the phone back into her pocket just as she got to Asher and Dare.

"Asher!"

No response.

Oh no!

"Asher!" she said louder, sliding down to her knees and shaking him. "Asher, you can't fall asleep. Nate and Hannah are twenty minutes away. I'm going to dig you out from under Dare and get you to the truck, okay? But you have to wake up. I can't carry you and I don't want to drag you."

She patted his cheeks.

Nothing.

No. Not like this.

She ripped down his buff and pressed her lips to his just as hot tears began to trickle down her cheeks.

"Not like this, you grumpy asshole. Not like this. I came back so that you could apologize to me *properly* and that means us, in bed, for hours. You owe me that. I'm a very forgiving person, but I still need some persuasion. And you're very good at that with your tongue."

She shook him by the shoulders.

Nothing.

Terror started a slow, lethal swirl in her gut that made her feel sick.

"Asher Harris, I will sit on your face right now if it will wake you up. I'm not fucking kidding." She pressed her mouth to his again and kissed him, sliding her tongue past his icy lips, breathing warm air into him.

Sobs shook her uncontrollably and tears slid down onto his face, but then, he started kissing her back.

He was kissing her back. Slowly, rigidly. But he was kissing her back and that was all that mattered.

"You're going to sit on my face?" he said when she pulled away, still crying.

"I will if it'll keep you awake."

His smile was small. "Might take me a while to get you there, but I'm game."

She chuckled through the blubbering and tears. "After. But right now, I need to dig you out. Stay the fuck awake, okay?"

"Mhmm."

She pulled the buff back over his mouth and nose, stood up, and started digging. The snow was wet and heavy, but eventually, she had dug out enough around Asher that when she went behind him, put her hands under his arms, and pulled, he budged.

"Oh thank God," she exhaled, slowly peeling him out from under Dare, though that seemed to cause the barbed wire to dig deeper into Dare and the horse let out a whimper of pain. "I'm sorry, buddy," she said. "I'm so sorry."

She got Asher free, then quickly checked him over. "Can you move your legs?" she asked. "Do they feel broken?"

He slowly lifted each leg, bending them at the knee. "Don't feel broken."

"Oh thank God." She started to drag him through the snow toward the truck. "Let me know if you can walk," she said to him.

He made a noise she didn't understand, but at least he was still making noises.

Sweat coated her forehead and her arms were threatening to give out, but she dug down deep for some extra energy and continued to lug his enormous frame to the truck.

Just when she thought she wasn't going to make it, bright high beams pierced through the darkness then a truck honked.

Nate.

Thank God.

The truck parked, leaving its lights on and a door opened then slammed shut.

Nate came running forward, his face painted with fear. "Holy fuck," he murmured, taking in Triss with Asher. Nate swooped in, picked up his brother, and carried him to Asher's truck, laying him on the back bench seat. "I've got spare blankets in my truck. Go grab all of them."

She nodded and took off.

Hannah's worried eyes meet her as she approached Nate's truck. Her friend rolled down the window. "How is he?"

Triss shook her head. "Not good. In and out of consciousness. But his legs aren't broken."

Hannah blew out a breath and nodded. "Silver lining, I guess."

Triss grabbed all of the blankets and even a couple of those shiny silver thermal blankets that were folded up under the seat. She raced back to Asher's truck where Nate had cranked the heat and was berating his brother.

"I told you not to do anything stupid," Nate said. "And then you went and did the stupidest fucking thing imaginable."

Asher's teeth were chattering, but already his lips had more color and his eyes were open wider.

"I'm nervous to leave him," Triss said. "But we need to go get Dare."

Nate seemed just as torn as she was. "We'll move him to my truck with Hannah, then she can keep an eye on him." He scooped Asher back up, blankets and all, and carried him effortlessly to the other truck where they cranked the heat and Hannah could talk his ear off and keep him awake.

"Should we get him to a hospital?" she asked.

Nate shook his head. "We should, but the closest hospital is in Denver, which is thirty minutes away and the roads are getting dicey again with all the snow. He fell through the ice of a frozen pond when we were kids on my uncle's ranch, I know what to do for hypothermia. As long as his legs aren't broken ..."

She shook her head. "They're not. We can assess him for spinal damage and further injuries when we get him home."

Nate nodded, then the two of them went to see about helping Dare.

She handed Nate the wire cutters and he clipped everything he could around Dare, then using the equine first aid kit from his truck, he bandaged up Dare's ankle. "Fuck, buddy," Nate said, petting the horse. "I don't want to put you down. I really don't."

"We're not going to," Triss said, glaring at Nate. "How do we get him into your truck and back to the barn?"

"This is a six-hundred-pound horse, Triss, we don't."

That wasn't the right answer.

She shook her head, unwilling to accept that this was Dare's fate. "We can call the vet. The road is clear enough still, one can come here and take a look, right?"

Nate shook his head. "I saw the break. The bones shattered and punctured through the skin. There is no coming back from this."

"You're giving up on him? He can come back. He can. He's strong, he's a fighter. You're just not willing to put in the work."

Nate's blue eyes held a hardness that sent up her hackles. "I'd spend every hour of my life fighting if I knew it would help this horse get better, but it won't. He'll get laminitis, possibly necrosis of the wound, and he'd have to stay laying down to recover, which will most likely mean pneumonia and pressure sores. We'd have to keep him constantly drugged and his life would be miserable. A break like this is fatal for a horse and every horse owner knows it. Asher knows it."

Fresh, hot tears spilled down her cheeks and her chin trembled. "So ... so what? You're just going to shoot him?"

His expression softened. "He's in pain right now, Triss. A lot of pain. The kindest thing to do right now is put him out of his misery. I hate that term, but it's true. Dare is scared, miserable and in agony. Nobody deserves that."

She shook her head. "He doesn't deserve to die like this."

"No horse does. This is one of the hardest parts about being a rancher, putting down your best friends."

Swallowing, she glanced over at Dare. "Does it have to be a gun?"

"I could drive back to the barn and get a sedative and the barbiturates the vet uses if you'd prefer. But I do have a gun in the truck. It would be faster and he would suffer less since it'd take time to drive back to the house. And he's already been in pain for a while."

"You're making this *my* decision?"

He shook his head. "No. I'm letting you know our choices, then we'll make the decision together. If you want me to euthanize him, I will. Or, you can go and hold him, pet him and tell him he's a good boy, then I'll do what needs to be done."

"What would Asher do?"

"The quickest and most painless way."

Sucking in a deep breath, she squeezed her eyes shut and nodded as more tears trailed down her cheeks. "Okay. Quick and painless."

He nodded and went to his truck, while she went over to Dare. Kneeling down in the snow, she pressed her forehead to the side of the horse's head. "I'm so sorry, Dare. I'm so, so sorry. You don't deserve this. None of us do."

She petted his velvety nose and kissed him, resting her head against his and scratching his ears.

Footsteps echoed, crunching through the snow and she glanced up to see Nate with the gun in his hand and regret on his face. His eyes were full of unshed tears and he swallowed hard. "I don't like this any more than you do," he said. "I probably hate it more because we've had Dare since we opened the ranch. He's a member of our family."

She nodded and choked as she tried to swallow past the razor blades in her throat. "I'm sorry you have to do this."

"It's part of being a rancher."

"Part of being a rancher," she repeated.

She kissed Dare again, whispered another apology, and stood up, turning her back to the horse, but jumping when a moment later the gunshot rang out through the eerily quiet night.

Her body shook and the tears continued to fall.

They fell for Dare, for Asher, for all of them.

How was Asher going to be when he realized his horse was dead? Was he going to blame himself? Was this going to be another trigger for him?

"I don't really want to leave a dead horse out in the snow," Nate said, approaching her. "But I can't do anything about it right now. I've got a tarp in the back of my truck, help me lay it over his body?"

Nodding, she stood stock-still until he returned with the big blue tarp, then robotically, she helped Nate drape the tarp over Dare's body, covering the edges of the tarp with snow to keep it down so the wind didn't lift it off.

Once all that could be done was done, Nate climbed into his truck and backed out onto the road. Triss didn't realize until then that he still had a small horse trailer hitched to the back. She climbed into Asher's truck and followed Nate to the farmhouse.

Together, they helped Asher, who was more conscious than earlier, into the house. She suggested the hot tub, but Nate said Asher needed to warm up slowly, otherwise he could go into shock if he went from freezing to boiling, so they'd have to wait before they brought him to the hot tub.

They checked him over, bandaged up some of his scrapes and scratches from the fence, double-checked he didn't break any bones, then got him into bed and covered him with blankets, an electric blanket, and hot water bottles. They also helped a cast-wearing Hannah into the house, where she took up roost on the couch and called the vet to make arrangements for tomorrow.

Triss felt like she'd aged ten years in a little over two hours.

Her eyes hurt when she tried to keep them open and her muscles ached. But it was her heart that felt tortured the most. Like someone had taken a railway spike and hammered it over and over again into the center of her ribcage.

"Go crawl into bed with Asher," Nate said, coming up to Triss where she stood in the kitchen, cradling her now cold mug of tea. She had no idea how long she'd been standing in front of the sink staring aimlessly out into the blackness of the backyard.

Nodding, but not saying anything, she took off up the stairs, peeled out of her wet clothes, and slid into the bed beside Asher, beneath all his blankets.

Gently, she placed her fingers to his neck to check his pulse. Steady and solid.

"I'm still alive," he croaked, peeling open one eye and rolling over to his side to face her, albeit with a fair bit of effort involved.

"How do you feel?"

"Alive," he repeated. "And like a horse fell on me. Just glad my legs and back aren't broken."

She smiled, though, it was a sad smile. "About Dare ..."

"I know," he said solemnly. "I knew pretty much the moment it happened."

"I'm so sorry." As if she hadn't cried enough already, fat tears blurred her vision and she had to bite her lip to keep it from trembling.

"I'm the sorry one. I never should have gone out in that. I know better. Dare deserved better." He swallowed and his eyes started to water. "I'm going to regret that for the rest of my life. Letting my anger and pain make me do a stupid, reckless stunt like that. I'm not fit to be a rancher. Not fit to be responsible for any life."

"Shhh," she cooed, snuggling up to him under the covers. "Those are the idiot thoughts talking."

"Huh?"

She wiped the tears from his cheeks and gazed up at him. "Well, you're not on drugs, so the only explanation is that you're an idiot and thinking stupid things."

He snorted and wrapped his arm around her, pulling him into his body. "Is that so?"

"Well, yeah, because only an idiot would tell me to leave."

"That's true."

"Only an idiot would think a couple of cracks and scratches means he's broken and useless."

"Well ..."

"*Only* an idiot," she confirmed. "Only an idiot would think that what we have is just a no-strings fling with zero feelings and that it could just be ended without anybody getting hurt. When in fact, I think *both* people got hurt more than they bargained for."

"That's true," he breathed out.

"Only an idiot would think that he's not fit to be a rancher when it's so clearly in every fiber of his being, what he was meant to be. And he should indeed be responsible for other lives."

He grunted.

She gripped his dog tags and tugged slightly to show him just how serious she was. "And only an idiot, would think that I'm not strong enough to stand at his side no matter what kind of shit life throws at him, no matter the triggers, the trauma, or the memories. You've got cracks, Asher, and maybe at one point you were broken, but you're not broken now. When I look at you, I don't see a broken man. I see a strong man with a story. And when you're ready—if you're ever ready—I'd like to hear that story so that I can better understand those cracks."

"You live in Connecticut," his voice was deep and hoarse and filled with emotion.

She nodded. "I do."

"And I live in Colorado."

"No, really?" She grinned at him.

He rolled his eyes but smiled. "How are we going to make this work?"

She shrugged. "We just do. We figure it out."

"Would you move here? Leave your job, your clients, your life?"

"I'm not attached to Connecticut and the town I live in. I moved there because I got a job offer after I graduated from grad school. The money was good. But there will always be jobs for speech paths no matter where I go. I'm not concerned about finding work. Worst case scenario, I start up my own practice and freelance. I know lots of people who do it and they get to set their own hours and pick their clients."

"We've been thinking about getting certified for therapeutic horse riding," he said. "Would there be any way we could link the two?"

"Asher Harris, are you asking me to start a business with you?"

"I'm asking you to move here, be with me, and that I'll support you in any way I can. If you want to start an entire therapy clinic here with speech paths, OTs, counselors, and therapists, I will make it happen. I will build you what you need and buy you the right horses for the job."

Her eyes went wide. "You've known me for six days."

Shoving his fingers into her hair, he held her head steady and pinned his gaze on her in that unwavering, solid way that had mesmerized her since the moment she met him. "And I'm ready to know you forever. It'll take time to sort everything out, but think about it. I'm going to go to counseling to work on my PTSD, and I'll get Nate to come with me to veteran's meetings. Whatever it takes. I never want to say goodbye to you again."

"Well, technically, you didn't even say *goodbye*, you just told me to leave."

"And I will never do that again." He eyes softened. Beautiful, blue orbs with unfathomable depth that had seen more despair than any person ever should. And yet, hope and love still burned bright inside them. Hope for the future. A future with her. "I'm sorry for the things I said and for telling you to go. It was the idiot thoughts. I had a lot of time to think while I was dying in the snow and I realized I've never been this happy in my life and I don't want this feeling to ever end."

This time they were tears of joy that burned her eyes as she blinked at him. "I haven't been this happy in a long time, either. But that's a big step after only six days."

"So we'll wait until the spring, but don't think this is the end of us, Triss, not by a fucking long shot."

Laughing, she cupped his face and pressed her lips to his. "I'm game. I don't want this feeling to end, either, so why should we let it?"

At that, he rolled on top of her, pinning her beneath his warm, solid frame. "Now, I'm sad but also happy, you're sad but also happy, and I'm pretty sure I have a lot of apologizing to do ... so ..."

She tapped him on the head and he grinned when he knew she was doing a subtle head push. "Then get apologizing, *cowboy*."

Epilogue

Two years later ...

"Ready?" Asher reached for his wife's hand and the two of them walked through the field toward the big Wasatch Maple at the back of the property.

They walked in silence, but it wasn't an uncomfortable silence. It was companionable.

She knew he wasn't always that big of a talker, and today, in particular, was a day of reflection.

When they reached the tree, Asher removed the small backpack from his back and opened it, unfurling a blanket and laying it down in the shade. He kneeled on it and offered Triss his hand, welcoming her to join him.

He situated her between his legs and they faced the tree and the five small headstones that spanned in front of the trunk.

"Well, Dare, old buddy ..." Asher said, forcing the words past his tight throat, "you're a daddy."

Triss turned her head and glanced up at him, kissing his jaw.

"Greenleigh delivered the first foal of the season. A little filly who we've named Daria, in honor of her dad. She's beautiful and perfect and looks just like you." He cleared his throat. "We're going to keep her and raise her to be a therapy horse for Triss's practice here on the ranch. Keep her in the family."

He hugged Triss tighter.

It'd been the glimmer of hope that he needed when the vet reminded him shortly after the accident with Dare, that they still had a few of Dare's specimens in the freezer at the clinic. So they waited until Greenleigh went into heat and then with their fingers crossed, hoped that the implantation took and they could continue Dare's legacy at the ranch.

And just last night little Daria was born, healthy, perfect and looking just like her sire.

They still had two more specimens at the clinic, so over the next few years, they planned to breed more little Dare Juniors to keep his memory alive and well.

Since starting the ranch, he and Nate had lost five horses, and each horse was cremated and their ashes spread beneath this tree where small headstones were placed. When he couldn't find his brother, but his truck was still in the yard, Asher knew Nate was probably out at the maple with the horses.

It was where Asher came, too, when the world got too loud.

"Mercy's foals with Callie and Hula-Hoop are due any day, too," Triss said. "We're going to have a field full of foals this summer." He loved that she was speaking to Dare, not to him. That she understood the importance in remembering the horses and not just dismissing them as "animals." They were their livelihood, their family, and their pets.

Even though he ate steak and bacon, Asher knew from the get-go that he could never raise cows or pigs for slaughter. He'd name them all, befriend them all and it would destroy him to put them down.

He'd be a shell of a human if he had to do that.

As it was, every time a horse died, a fragment of his heart went with it. He couldn't imagine having to kill over and over again and what that would do to him. He'd done enough of that in Iraq to last a lifetime.

"So ... Dare, we have some news," Triss started, snuggling deeper into Asher's embrace. "You're a daddy, but Asher is also going to be a daddy."

Asher leaped up from his spot on the blanket, which caused Triss to fall backward.

"Oh shit," he said, dropping back down to his knees. "I'm sorry."

"It's okay." Her tinkling laugh sent ribbons of warmth spinning through him. They wrapped around his heart and squeezed. She sat up, her smile big and beautiful. Suddenly the entire day seemed brighter. His life seemed brighter.

"Are you serious?" he asked taking her hand. "You're pregnant?"

They'd been trying for about six months, but so far hadn't had any luck. He'd given up hope, wondering if it was the universe's way of telling him he wasn't unbroken enough to be a parent.

She nodded, tears filling up her eyes, but she just kept smiling. "I am. Doctor confirmed it this morning."

His brain and heart felt like they were going to explode. He couldn't remember ever being this happy.

He turned back to the tree and focused on Dare's headstone. "You hear that, buddy? I'm going to be a dad, just like you."

Triss laughed and when he turned back to face her, tears streamed down her flushed cheeks.

"How are you feeling?" he asked. "When did you ..."

He had a million questions, and he knew without a doubt that his patient and kind woman would sit and answer every single one if he needed her to.

"My boobs hurt, I'm tired and a little nauseous. It was why I booked an appointment with my doctor when I went to Denver earlier today for that meeting with the school board. Figured I may as well kill two birds with one stone. I had suspicions that I might be. And Pasha said that those were definite signs of being pregnant. But I didn't want to get your hopes up until it was confirmed. But … " She shrugged. "It's confirmed. We're going to have a little cowboy or cowgirl in about eight months."

"Rancher," he corrected, dropping his brows and mouth into a scowl for a half-second, before breaking into a big grin again.

"Right, rancher."

"So eight months?" he asked, sitting back down to face the tree and drawing her into his embrace again between his legs. His palms fell to her flat stomach and her hands covered his. "About that. I'm roughly five weeks along. So … baby will be born late January. But an ultrasound will give us a more definitive date."

"And when do we get one of those?"

"We'll have one around eleven weeks, when they can hear the heartbeat, then another around twenty weeks, which is when we can find out if we're having a cowboy or cowgirl."

"Rancher."

She giggled. She loved to tease him and call him cowboy, even though if someone else called him cowboy, she was the first to correct them and say he was a rancher.

"Do you want to find out?" he asked.

She shrugged. "I'm open to the surprise, or to finding out. We can make that decision closer to the day. Though, on my drive home today I kept envisioning a little girl with wild, dark wavy hair like mine and bright blue eyes like yours running through the field with the goats and an enormous grin on her face." He could hear the smile in her voice. "But then I also saw a little boy with dark hair and blue eyes in overalls using an overturned bucket to climb into the goat stall and get up to all kinds of mischief."

"Well, we're definitely not stopping at one kid. So with any luck, we'll have both of those kids. Or, we'll have a house full of boys, or a house full of girls."

"Which we will definitely not raise the way my parents raised their house full of girls."

"And, I got guns and acreage where they'll never find the bodies."

"Of our children?" she asked, shock in her voice as she craned her neck around to face him, horror in her brown eyes.

He shook his head and grinned. "No, of the people that try to hurt them."

"Oh." She nodded and turned back to face the tree. "And I'm very good at shoveling."

"That you are." Chuckling, he pried his hands out from beneath hers and gently, this time, slid back from where he sat. He laid her down on the blanket and covered her with his body. "This won't hurt the baby?"

She grinned up at him and looped her arms around his neck. "Not in the slightest. Happy mom, happy baby. And *this* makes mom *very* happy."

He cradled her face in his hands, brushing her wild hair off her cheeks. "You make me happy. This life makes me happy and the fact that we're having a baby, I didn't think I could ever *be* this happy."

Her swallow was hard and fresh tears welled up in her eyes. "Me too. I love you, cowboy."

He smiled down at her. "And I love you, and I always will."

Grab the bonus scene here: https://whitleycox.com/bonus-rancher

If you've enjoyed this book, please consider leaving a review wherever you purchased it. It really does make a difference and helps an independent author like me.

Thank you again.

Xoxo

Whitley Cox

WHITLEY
COX

Check out the next Young Sidster Novel Coming May 2023

Preorder it here —>

https://mybook..to/second-chance-rancher

Second Chance with the Rancher

Mieka and Nate

Coming May 13, 2023

Preorder here—> https://mybook..to/second-chance-rancher

CHAPTER ONE

"Stupid piece of shit Ford," Nate muttered, as he hunched over even more under the hood of his pickup to get closer to the problem. "Found on road dead. Fix or repair daily. Stupid fucking piece of shit." He let out another string of colorful words that would probably make a sailor turn scarlet in mortification when the crunch of gravel broke through his soliloquy of swear words. He didn't recognize the sound of that vehicle's engine, and normally he could tell which truck or car was ambling down the long drive of the ranch just by the engine and the way the tires rumbled over the gravel.

No riding tours were on the books for today, and they hadn't officially opened the petting farm on weekdays yet. They'd do that next week once all the kids got out of school for the summer. It was nearly the end of May and although the mornings and evenings were still cool, the days had already grown hot and sweat beaded on his brow like a string of salty pearls.

It was probably just one of the many families that paid to board their horse on the ranch. They made a sweet killing by offering up stables to those who wanted horses but had nowhere to keep them. The weekends were busier, of course, but there was usually one or two owners milling around, brushing their horse or taking it for a ride.

He lifted his head to greet the new arrival only to bash it mighty hard on the inside of the hood.

"Jesus Christ, motherfucking piece of shit! Fuck!" He closed his eyes and rubbed his head. He'd have a goose egg for sure.

The vehicle came to a stop.

A door opened. Another door opened but only one closed. There were voices. A man and a woman. Then feet on the gravel followed by another door closing and tires spinning in the gravel as the car—he'd determined quickly that it was a car, not a truck—turned around and headed back toward the main road.

Still rubbing his head from where he'd smashed it against the hood, he squinted into the afternoon sun at the tall, slim figure walking gracefully toward him.

Shielding his eyes with his hand—even though he didn't have to, he knew that walk and those hips well—he sucked in a sharp breath and watched Mieka Young walk toward him, awkwardly pulling a suitcase behind her with one hand, while her other arm and wrist were in a cast.

Help her, you dumbass.

As if smacked in the back of the head by an imaginary Nana somewhere, he shook his head to free the cannoning thoughts that had left him paralyzed and raced forward. "Let me help you."

Mieka smiled shyly. "Thank you."

His heart lurched in his chest. It'd been a while since he'd seen her. And the last time that he had it'd been under unusual and *difficult* circumstances. Unusual and difficult circumstances were the result of the *previous* time they'd seen each other.

"How are you?" she asked, her full lips pulling sideways into a small, awkward smile.

"Busy," he said, doing everything he could to slow down his heart rate. His knuckles ached from how tightly he was squeezing the handle of her suitcase. He needed to calm the fuck down.

"Never a moment's rest when you run a ranch I suppose," she said, throwing in a girly chuckle.

"Nope."

Casting her honey-brown eyes around the big open driveway that separated the main barn from the farmhouse, she cradled her broken arm against her abdomen and allowed her shoulders to droop. "Is my sister around?"

"Triss and Ash are out in the back field. They've gone to give Dare some news. He's a daddy. Little Daria was born last night."

Her eyes perked up. "A new foal?"

Nate nodded and his pulse relaxed a bit. Anything to do with horses eased his troubles, and right now, he was troubled. "Wanna come see?"

Her smile was big and bright and only added to her incredible beauty.

He tucked her suitcase next to his truck and jerked his head toward the barn just as a series of barks erupted from the south side of the barn. A moment later, Nate's Blue Merle Aussie Shepherd, Bruno came racing around the corner, his tongue lolling out the side of his smiling mouth. He recognized Mieka right away and zoomed up to her.

"Hello, Bruno," Mieka said, pausing to bend down and pet Bruno who was lapping up her affection like he hadn't been given any attention in a month. "I love his different-colored eyes," she said. "They're so cool."

"It's why I picked him," Nate murmured, waiting until Mieka and Bruno got reacquainted and the dog stopped trying to smother her with love and kisses.

Eventually, Bruno settled down and the three of them were able to get back to their task of going to check out the new foal.

Curiosity burned hot inside him as he tossed some side-eyed glances toward the brown-haired beauty. What was she doing here? Did Triss know she was coming? Was it as awkward for her as it was for him? How long was she staying?

He opened the side door for the barn and allowed her to walk through first. He tried hard not to inhale when she walked past him, but it was fucking impossible. Her coconut shampoo went straight up his nose and made a beeline for his balls. Fuck.

"Which mare did Dare have a foal with?" she asked, turning to look up at him with those gold-flecked brown eyes of hers he'd gotten lost in one night after days of flirting and stolen glances.

Nate cleared his throat. "Greenleigh. Moved her to a bigger stall since there are two of them now. They're down at the end."

Mieka nodded and continued on down the barn, petting the cheeks and long faces of each horse she passed. She was a lot like her older sister, both women seemed to be naturals with animals. It was one of the things that had drawn him to Mieka in the first place. She had a wildness about her, but as much as she was wild, she was also soft and gentle. Which was something animals—particularly horses—needed.

She poked her head over into two adjacent stalls. "These mamas look ready to pop, too."

"Callie and Hula-Hoop are due with Mercy's foals any day," he replied.

"Oh, how fun. A field full of foals for the summer."

She reached Greenleigh's stall and peered over the side where Greenleigh was busy nursing a healthy little filly they'd named Daria after her late father—Dare. Dare had been Asher's horse, but after a freak accident a couple of winters back, Dare had fallen into a gopher hole in the snow, broke his leg and they were forced to put the gentle giant down. That was where Triss and Asher were right now, telling Dare's ashes under the old maple tree that he was a daddy.

"She's beautiful," Mieka cooed, opening up the stable door without asking and stepping inside. Bruno nudged Nate's leg and Nate bent down and gave his trusty companion a thorough scratch behind the ears while eying the slim dancer as she cautiously made her way to the side of Greenleigh's head. "Hello, lovely mama. What a gorgeous little girl you have. Dare would be so proud, I'm sure." She scratched the long bridge of Greenleigh's nose until Daria stopped nursing and came over to sniff and check out Mieka, too. She nudged her a couple of times, pulling a laugh from Mieka, who eventually petted the foal, too. "Brazen little thing, hmm?"

"We're going to keep her and raise her to be a therapy horse for the clinic," Nate said, hating the awkward silence between them and feeling the need to keep talking like an idiot.

"That's a great idea. Triss said business is booming and the waitlist is getting longer by the day. It'll be great if you can offer therapeutic riding and camps for special needs kids and stuff." She wasn't looking at him, but rather giving all of her attention to the horses.

"That's the plan."

"Well, I'd love to help out any way I can with the upcoming other births." She finally turned to face him. "That is, if you *need* help."

"Can always use another set of hands during a birth. Can always use another set of hands on the ranch."

He glanced out one of the barn windows to see Triss and Asher making their way back hand-in-hand through the field. Several horses were grazing and he could hear their hired ranch hands feeding the chickens, mucking stalls and tending to the goats. A couple of other hands were out riding the fence looking for holes, and two home schooled teenage girls whose parents paid for their horses to be boarded at the ranch, were in the outside coral practicing jumps. It was a weekday so things were quiet. It was the weekends and when summer was in full swing that things got hairy. Multiple dude ranch guided rides a day, the petting farm would open up soon, and all the kids with boarded horses would be around riding as much as they could while school wasn't in session.

It was their best money-making time, but it was also insane and they really could use all the help they could get.

She lifted her casted arm. "Not sure how much help I'll be, but I'll do what I can."

"What happened?" he asked, holding open the stall door so that she could step back out. Macklin, the attention-whore horse who would literally try to sit in your lap if you sat down in his stall made huffs and brays of frustration that he hadn't been given love yet, so Mieka made her way over to his stall, nuzzling him as soon as she got there.

"It was stupid, really. My own fault."

He waited for her to elaborate.

"I'm not a spring chicken anymore and can't do the moves I used to do in my teens and twenties." Her face fell and she kissed Macklin's cheek. "I did a flip and went to land on one hand—something I've done, or *did* thousands of times before—but this was a new routine and I was out of practice. My arm twisted, which messed with my balance, then I fell funny and snapped my radius."

"Fuck," he murmured.

"Yeah."

"How long are you out of commission?"

Her bottom lip wobbled for a moment, then she huffed out a sarcastic one-breath laugh. "Well, that depends who you talk to. My doctor says I'll be in a cast for six to eight weeks. I might be able to get an air cast sooner if the healing is quick. I've got about six screws and two plates in it which will speed up the healing. But if you ask our choreographer and the manager of the dance company I was with on the cruise ship, my career is over."

"What?" Anger lashed through him. "You broke your arm, not your ankle or hip."

"Thirty-four is old for a cruise ship dancer. They're surprised I've lasted this long without breaking something. My contract was up and they took this *break* as an opportunity not to renew with me."

A red-hot heat wormed its way through Nate's body. "You've got to be kidding me?"

Tears welled up in Mieka's eyes and her throat bobbed on a harsh swallow. "That's what I said. But nope. So, I'm jobless, homeless—since I lived out of a suitcase on the ships for years, and—" she lifted up her casted arm, "literally broken." She sucked in a rattled breath and it looked as if she was about to breakdown into sobs, but Triss's voice interrupted them and caused Mieka to sober, wipe her eyes and throw on a big smile.

"Mieka?" Triss said.

"Hey, sis," Mieka said, grinning.

"I ... this is a surprise." The sisters embraced, but Triss cast a curious glance at Nate over Mieka's shoulder. "Is everything okay?" They broke their embrace and Triss's gaze fell to Mieka's casted right arm. "Oh my God, what happened?"

"Spring chickens are made of rubber, old stewing hens like me are apparently made of porcelain and break easily." Her tone was full of anger and sarcasm and Nate one hundred percent understood why.

"Huh?" Triss glanced at her husband, then at Nate, her brown eyes—the same gold-flecked shade as Mieka's narrowing in confusion."

"I did a move I'd done a million times when I wasn't a washed up old hag and my brittle bones couldn't handle it, so they shattered like fine crystal on a tile floor," Mieka said. "Now, I'm jobless, homeless and according to my asshole choreographer *Martin*, I'm also washed up."

"What the fuck?" Asher muttered. "He said that?"

"Martin has no filter," Mieka replied.

"We have a baby sister like that, but even she wouldn't be so mean as to call you—or anyone *washed up*. A broken arm does not mean you're incapable. It will heal and you can go back to dancing on the ships, right?" Triss, rubbed her sister's back affectionately.

Mieka sniffed and shook her head. "They wouldn't renew my contract. I'm old."

"Oh my God, you're not *old*. You're thirty-four. That's *not* old." Triss rolled her eyes. "They're idiots. You'll get hired on by another cruise line no problem, I know it."

Uncertainly shimmered in Mieka's eyes, along with fresh unshed tears. As much as she hoped her sister was right, Nate could see that Mieka was convinced her dancing days on the luxury cruise ships were over.

Nate knew nothing of that world or industry, so he wasn't planning to weigh in, but the pure look of defeat and sadness in Mieka's eyes had his protective instincts kicking in. He was a fixer. He fixed things. Broken vehicles, injured animals, rickety fences. He fixed.

But a sad woman—who he had carnal knowledge of—was a completely different thing and he wasn't sure he even knew where to begin when it came to mending her broken heart and tattered spirit. He sure as hell wanted to try, though.

"So, I'm here to drink until I forget how to dance, cuddle foals and bake bread, or pies or whatever. Put me to work. I don't know how much good I'll be mucking stalls and stuff with only one arm, but I'm happy and willing to pitch in wherever I can. And we can get shitfaced every night and talk trash about our parents and Royal Olympian Cruise Line."

Triss's mouth twisted in a funny way and she cast a cursory glance at Asher who shoved his hands deep into the pockets of his jeans, then rocked back on his heels. "I um ... I won't be getting shitfaced with you, unfortunately," Triss said.

Mieka studied her sister in confusion for half a second, then her eyes went wide. It took Nate a couple more seconds to clue in, but then he did too, his eyes shot to his brother who was all cocky grins.

"A baby?" Nate asked, all excited.

Asher smiled wide.

"We're going to have a little cowboy or cowgirl," Triss said softly, resting her hand on her flat belly.

"Rancher," Asher corrected.

Triss smiled and rolled her eyes. "Right, rancher."

Mieka swallowed, blinked and forced the fakest smile Nate had ever seen on anybody ever. "That's amazing. I'm so happy for you." Then she threw herself at her sister and hugged her tight.

When they broke their embrace this time, Mieka was teary-eyed, so she wiped her fingers beneath her eyes and smiled. "This calls for a celebration. You might not be able to drink, but I sure can." She turned to Nate and Asher. "Boys, don't make me drink alone."

"I've got some stuff to do in the barn still," Asher said.

Mieka turned to Nate. "Nate?"

It was only four o'clock in the afternoon, he still had shit to do, too, and his truck was still making that weird clunking sound and he hadn't been able to figure out where the problem was. But the look of pure desperation in Mieka's eyes tugged at his heart until he thought it might be ripped clean from his chest, so he nodded. "Sure."

She beamed, but it was all fake. "Excellent." Then she linked arms with her sister and the two of them headed off toward the house through the barn.

Asher turned to Nate. "A little early to start drinking."

"She's in pain," he said plainly.

"From her arm? Can't she just take some ibuprofen? I'm sure the doctor prescribed her some fun painkillers like T3s or oxy."

"Not her arm," he said, shaking his head as he watched the two women continue to walk away. "It's her heart." And he was determined to find a way to fix it, even if it broke his own in the process.

Preorder here—>https://mybook..to/second-chance-rancher

ACKNOWLEDGMENTS

There are so many people to thank who help along the way. Publishing a book is definitely not a solo mission, that's for sure.

Thank you to my editor Proofreading by the Page. Excellent job. I really appreciate your hard work and feedback.

Megan J. Parker-Squiers from EmCat Designs, your covers are awesome. This cover is exactly what I wanted and so freaking beautiful. You knocked it out of the park! Thank you.

My reader group, Whitley Cox's Fabulously Filthy Reviewers, you are all awesome and I feel so blessed to have found such wonderful fans.

Author Brooke Burton with Positive Proof author services. Thank you so much for your beta read. You just get me, girl. You really do. Your feedback is positive but constructive and so freaking helpful. Plus, when you send me memes and GIFS to brighten my day it makes all the difference. I don't know what I did to deserve your friendship, but I'm so grateful for it.

My assistant Meghan Macphail with Kiss my Smut, I could not function without you. You take care of all the stuff I don't want to do so I can focus on what I love which is writing. You are an angel and gem and a true blessing. Thank you!!!!

Author Ember Leigh, my newest author bestie, I love our bitch fests—they keep me sane.

My parents and brother, thank you for your unwavering support. The Small Human and the Tiny Human, you are the beats and beasts of my heart, the reason I breathe and the reason I drink. I love you both to infinity and beyond. And lastly, of course, the husband. You are my forever, my other half, the one who keeps me grounded and the only person I have honestly never grown sick of even when we did that six-month backpacking trip and spent every single day together. I never tired of you. Never needed a break. You are my person. I love you.

Website: WhitleyCox.com
Email: readers4wcox@gmail.com
Twitter: @WhitleyCoxBooks
Instagram: @CoxWhitley
TikTok: @AuthorWhitleyCox
Facebook : https://www.facebook.com/CoxWhitley/
Blog: https://whitleycox.com/fabulously-filthy-blog-page/

Exclusive Facebook Reader Group:
https://www.facebook.com/groups/234716323653592/
Booksprout: https://booksprout.co/author/994/whitley-cox
Bookbub: https://www.bookbub.com/authors/whitley-cox
Goodreads:
https://www.goodreads.com/author/show/16344419.Whitley_Cox
Subscribe to my newsletter here:
http://eepurl.com/ckh5yT

ABOUT THE AUTHOR

A Canadian West Coast baby born and raised, Whitley is married to her high school sweetheart, and together they have two beautiful daughters and a fluffy dog. She spends her days making food that gets thrown on the floor, vacuuming Cheerios out from under the couch and making sure that the dog food doesn't end up in the air conditioner. But when the kids are at school, and it's not quite wine o'clock, Whitley sits down, avoids the pile of laundry on the couch, and writes.

A lover of all things decadent; wine, cheese, chocolate and spicy erotic romance, Whitley brings the humorous side of sex, the ridiculous side of relationships and the suspense of everyday life into her stories. With single dads, firefighters, Navy SEALs, mommy wars, body issues, threesomes, bondage and role-playing, Whitley's books have all the funny and fabulously filthy words you could hope for.

OTHER BOOKS BY WHITLEY COX

Love, Passion and Power: Part 1
The Dark and Damaged Hearts Series: Book 1
https://books2read.com/LPP1-DDH
Kendra and Justin

•

Love, Passion and Power: Part 2
The Dark and Damaged Hearts: Book 2
https://books2read.com/LPP2-DDH
Kendra and Justin

•

Sex, Heat and Hunger: Part 1
The Dark and Damaged Hearts Book 3
https://books2read.com/SHH1-DDH
Emma and James

•

Sex, Heat and Hunger: Part 2
The Dark and Damaged Hearts Book 4
https://books2read.com/SHH1-DDH
Emma and James

•

Hot & Filthy: The Honeymoon
The Dark and Damaged Hearts Book 4.5
https://books2read.com/HF-DDH
Emma and James

•

True, Deep and Forever: Part 1
The Dark and Damaged Hearts Book 5
https://books2read.com/TDF1-DDH
Amy and Garrett

•

True, Deep and Forever: Part 2
The Dark and Damaged Hearts Book 6
https://books2read.com/TDF2-DDH
Amy and Garrett

190

•

Hard, Fast and Madly: Part 1
The Dark and Damaged Hearts Series Book 7
https://books2read.com/HFM1-DDH
Freya and Jacob
•

Hard, Fast and Madly: Part 2
The Dark and Damaged Hearts Series Book 8
https://books2read.com/HFM1-DDH
Freya and Jacob
•

Quick & Dirty
Book 1, A Quick Billionaires Novel
https://books2read.com/QDirty-QBS
Parker and Tate
•

Quick & Easy
Book 2, A Quick Billionaires Novella
https://books2read.com/QEasy-QBS
Heather and Gavin
•

Quick & Reckless
Book 3, A Quick Billionaires Novel
https://books2read.com/QReckless-QBS
Silver and Warren
•

Quick & Dangerous
Book 4, A Quick Billionaires Novel
https://books2read.com/QDangerous-QBS
Skyler and Roberto
•

Quick & Snowy
The Quick Billionaires, Book 5
https://books2read.com/QSnowy-QBS
Brier and Barnes
•

Doctor Smug
https://books2read.com/DoctorSmug
Daisy and Riley
•

WHITLEY COX

Hot Dad
https://books2read.com/Hot-Dad
Harper and Sam
•
Snowed In & Set Up
https://books2read.com/SISU
Amber, Will, Juniper, Hunter, Rowen, Austin
•
Love to Hate You
https://books2read.com/Love2HateYou
Alex and Eli
•
Lust Abroad
https://books2read.com/Lust-Abroad
Piper and Derrick
•
Hired by the Single Dad
https://books2read.com/HBTSD-SDS
The Single Dads of Seattle, Book 1
Tori and Mark
•
Dancing with the Single Dad
https://books2read.com/DWTSD-SDS
The Single Dads of Seattle, Book 2
Violet and Adam
•
Saved by the Single Dad
https://books2read.com/SBTSD-SDS
The Single Dads of Seattle, Book 3
Paige and Mitch
•
Living with the Single Dad
https://books2read.com/LWTSD-SDS
The Single Dads of Seattle, Book 4
Isobel and Aaron
•
Christmas with the Single Dad
https://books2read.com/CWTSD-SDS
The Single Dads of Seattle, Book 5
Aurora and Zak

Snowed in with the Rancher
A Young Sisters Novel
https://books2read.com/snowed-in-rancher
Triss and Asher
March 4, 2023

•

Second Chance with the Rancher
A Young Sisters Novel
https://books2read.com/second-chance-rancher
Mieka and Nate
May 13, 2023

•

Done with You
A Young Sisters Novel
https://books2read.com/done-with-you
Oona and Aiden
October 13, 2023

•

Rock the Shores
A Cinnamon Bay Romance
https://books2read.com/Rocktheshores
Juliet and Evan

•

The Bastard Heir
Winter Harbor Heroes, Book 1
Co-written with Ember Leigh
https://books2read.com/the-bastard-heir
Harlow and Callum

•

The Asshole Heir
Winter Harbor Heroes, Book 2
Co-written with Ember Leigh
https://books2read.com/the-asshole-heir
Amaya and Carson

The Rebel Heir
Winter Harbor Heroes, Book 3
Co-written with Ember Leigh
https://books2read.com/the-rebel-heir
Lily and Colton
March 18, 2023

NATALIE SLOAN TITLES

Light the Fire
Revolution Inferno, Book 1
https://mybook.to/light-the-fire
Haina, Zane, Alaric and Jorik

•

Stoke the Flames
Revolution Inferno, Book 2
https://mybook.to/stoke-the-flames
Olia, Maxxon, Cypher and Alaric

•

Burn it Down
Revolution Inferno, Book 3
https://mybook.to/burn-it-down
Zosha, Knox, Shade and Tozer
June 3, 2023